Beth,

BURNING GOLD

by Clea Calloway

Stay Inspired!

Clea

Cover adapted from original work by See Me Design

Printed in the United States of America.
For information address Clea Was Here, LLC, 1266 W. Paces Ferry Road, Suite 272, Atlanta, Georgia, 30327.

Library of Congress Control Number: 2013920644

ISBN: 978-0-9886296-0-8
eISBN: 978-0-9886296-1-5

For information regarding special discounts for bulk purchases please contact
Clea Was Here, LLC, cleacallowayatl@gmail.com
Or visit my website at www.Cleacalloway.com

To my editors and manuscript evaluators, many thanks for your patience! To Tom Bird for teaching me how to write a book. To my self-proclaimed Godmother, Barbara Lebow, whose encouragement from the outset has been my strength. To my friends, for holding a place for me at our lunches. I'll be back! To my family, who still smiled and thanked me despite the countless cold sandwich dinners and lack of milk in the fridge, you cannot be appreciated enough. To my husband, Marcus, the man who makes all of my dreams possible. If I had it to do all over again, I'd do it with you.

This book is dedicated to my daughters, Amanda, Amelia, and Alyssa, who inspire me each and every day.
You can do anything you set your mind to do. Believe.

In memory of my Mother,
Michele Rubin McNichols.
Thank you for always keeping your love strong and your heart open.

Jenni Ann

Age Four

As I ran way ahead of Pappy and Nana, I heard the warning shouted out to me: "Don't go any farther than the top, Little Nugget! Wait for us there!"

"Okay Pappy!" I shouted back, still running. I wanted to be the first one to see the top. I had heard them talk about how beautiful it is and I was determined to see it first. The rhododendron hung low - it sometimes slapped my face as I raced by. I had to hop up on some mossy green rocks to get past the muddy puddle in the middle of the trail. The damp coolness at the trailhead below gave way to warm sunshine and buzzing bees as I ran higher and higher up the mountain.

Finally, I could see the railing on my left. It stood there old and rotting, a faded beauty queen, a feeble warning. I got closer peering out onto the vastness that is the North Georgia Mountains. It is as though I had never seen a color before that day. The mountain tops were waves in a choppy ten-foot sea swell, never-ending, with a bounty of glorious colors, each playing vividly upon the other. The steady beat of my heart slowed. The scene was calming. I planned calling out, "King of the Hill!" when I got to the top. But I stood there, speechless, mesmerized by the lushness of the fall colors. A large red tailed hawk sailed past in a sweep of brown against the ruby and gold leaves below. They are jewels, these colors.

"Pappy?" I asked when they got there. "Why don't my crayons look like these colors?"

"Well you see Little Nugget," he replied. "These here colors, these are real special. These are made by God's crayons."

As we looked out at the sea of color surrounding us, I repeated out loud in wonder, "God's crayons."

~~~

Age Twenty

Driving, driving, speeding fast, the green Miata convertible is taking the curves of the North Georgia Mountains well, so much so that car, driver and road act as one. A few leaves place a glancing blow on the windshield. Now a large yellow maple leaf smacks it hard and is quickly ripped away by the wind as I take another curve. As pieces of my hair slip out of the clip holding it back, I slow, but just a bit. My red wool blend scarf has been waving to all who will see as I pass by. This is where I belong.

Fall has no better place to be than with me in these mountains. I take the final turn on a gravel road, slowing, slowing. The old homeplace is here. Here is where my great-grandparents bought the land, back in 1937, the year my Pappy was born. The simple shack they lived in serves as the garden shed out back now. The homeplace I know, the one that sits before me, is the one my Pappy built. He felled, cut, and sanded the knotty heart of pine that makes up each and every one of the ceiling beams. We didn't have any other grandpappy. Or any other grandparents at all that we ever knew. Just the homeplace and Nana and Pappy Gold.

I get waves of warmth just remembering his strong arms lifting me and my sister when we came for a visit. He was a garrulous man, with great height and powerful strength. And the bluest eyes – they sparkled like diamonds bursting out of a deep Aegean sea. Those eyes shone so bright, a beaming really, as if no one loved you more and nothing bad could ever happen to you, ever.

My sister, Abby, and I could just about do anything we wanted to up there. For others, he put up with no slack and rewards were few. You were expected to pull your weight and then some if needed. I'll never forget one rainy afternoon when I must have been eight or maybe nine years old. The heavy humid heat had made its way up the piedmont to the North Georgia Mountains from the plateau below. Sweat was pouring off of Pappy's brow, mixing with the rain so you didn't know which was which.

"Shovel that damn mud out before it slides down the hill!" he was screaming through the waves of the water that were slapping the ground, equaling the force of his voice. I had been included on this ride to bring the goods to market, but we hadn't made it far before a torrential rain sprang up. It was unexpected and violent, leaving the road ahead partially washed out with us stuck on the edge. As I stood, wet and scared on the side of an uphill bank where Pappy put me, I heard the exchange.

"But Mr. Gold, Sir," whined the newly hired hand, "we've been at this for almost an hour and I am so tired!"

"Now look here son," he demanded as he strode over to the other side of the truck, filled with chickens. "There is no time for your belly-aching. Move the hell over and give me that shovel. Turner!" he hollered through the squawking of our merchandise to his long time faithful employee. Turner was straining to keep the front side of the truck wedged with a chock of wood, found fortuitously nearby when the truck started its precarious decent sideways down the muddy roadway.

"Yes Sir!" answered Turner who knew when to mess with Pappy, and this was most definitely not the time.

"Turner, take this rope from me and tie it across the road to that tree. While you're at it, see if you can get pansy boy here to help you hold it while I dig this wheel out!"

It occurs to Turner that he doesn't even know this new boy's name. But he knows there's no need. He knows this kid will be gone by dawn. And indeed he was right.

Pappy thought the new youth was soft, clumsy, and not hard-working enough. No one worked harder than Pappy did, no one in the whole state – no siree. He was tough and had everything it took to back it up. As tough as he was, he was equally in full and open love with his family. Pappy said he knew when he began working this land, when he was just a teenager himself, that it was where his family would be born and raised. He knew that this is where he wanted to live and die.

Driving up the road, now re-built with a much smoother combination of crushed rock, gravel and dirt, I get a glimpse of the homeplace. I drive all the way up, past the house, down the knoll, to visit my beloved Pappy. Closer to the creek that leads into the pond, under Old Maple, as he used to call the tree, is the headstone for him and my Nana where they lie. I get out smiling and sweep some of the parched golden leaves away, just enough to see their names.

"Hello Nana and Pappy," I say aloud. Just their memory brings me the familiar calm I need so much.

Pappy was my mother's father. She, too, was like him. Hard working, no-nonsense, good-hearted. I work hard too. I am an artist, painting mostly, oil on canvas. I dabbled in sculpture, but it felt like construction work, the wood, the metals, just not for me. No, I was meant for the easel. And the oil. I could paint still life and city scenes but landscapes were where my heart lay.

One of my pieces is a scene scape with craggy rocks and rough-hewn trees, scaling up towards the cliff's edge, where you see the ghostly outline of a couple, a man and a woman, and a child, a little girl. The man and woman are holding hands with their heads tilted towards each other, the woman's slightly facing upwards as if smelling the salt coming off the raging ocean below. The girl, holding her mother's hand, with her head and upper body leaning into her mother's side, is just balancing on the one left foot, looking down. This is my family.

~~~

Age Five

"Now, Jenni!" my daddy called out to me. He released his grip from the back of my seat cushion. The wheels turn as I steer. I lurch from side to side. The shiny pink tassels sprouting from my handlebars are playfully chasing my every move.

"Now, just pedal," he coaches.

"You can do it!" he says again, more enthusiastically. I lope left and then a bit too far right before I am able to straighten and pedal.

"You're doing it Jenni Ann, you're riding a bike!"

I am five years old. The training wheels are newly removed, and my first big lesson of facing my fears is upon me. But *look at me*! I am riding this bike! It takes a few more tries for me to get started by myself, without Daddy's help. But I don't want him to leave. I want him to stay and watch me ride in circles again and again.

I'm not sure who he is more proud of that day, him or me. Earlier, Mom had said, "Trey, you're going to get her killed. It is too soon for her to ride without her training wheels." Her green eyes would show fire while the soft creases around them that had begun to form belied her concerns. Mom was always the worrier.

"Lori, honey!" Daddy roars. "Come out here and see your baby now! Come see your baby girl ride that bike! She's a natural!"

Mom comes out, applauds and smiles broadly. As I am pedaling back towards them both, grinning like a Cheshire cat, I can see Daddy reach up. He takes her chin so lightly and kisses her gently on the lips. I circle around them, almost falling, as they break away from each other and cheer me on—as if I'd just discovered the cure for some dreaded disease. We were so happy.

~~~

Will Hardy

Age Five

I was sent to the neighbors for another sleepover. My mother was crying again. At first I couldn't understand. But sitting in the living room I overheard Mrs. Crowder telling Mr. Crowder.

"She should just be happy with the one she has!"

"Ummm-hum," mumbled Mr. Crowder.

"I mean, all that bed rest, and still look what happens! I really do feel sorry for her but...I mean...it just keeps her from taking care of her own. That's all."

Mr. Crowder mumbled something again.

"What would she do without our Christian generosity? That's all I'm saying," she said over the clattering of dishes.

"Yes, dear," replied Mr. Crowder.

"William!" she called out. "Dinner's ready. Come get your plate!"

As I sat alone in front of the television eating boiled hot dogs and peas I pondered what she had said. I tiptoed around my house because of mother. Let her rest, Daddy had said. I knew mother wanted a baby. But wasn't I enough? Maybe I wasn't making her happy! I was determined to be a better boy so mother wouldn't be so sad. Maybe then she would play with me again! Maybe she would take me to the park and she would push me in the swing! And she would laugh as I jumped from my seat tumbling to the ground like a high-flying trapeze artist! Yes, I would be better. And everything would go back to the way it was. Everyone would be happy.

~~~

Jenni Ann

Age Twenty

I would come up to the homeplace alone more and more. Walking around the pond I watched as the ducks and geese vie for their places. I pull the old silver canoe out from under the pond's dock and, joining them, paddle quietly alongside.

I long to see the big black dog named Minnie that could nearly whip us to the ground with her wagging tail, and the other shorter legged mutt named Racer that spent most of his time lying about. Pappy had a keen sense of humor and the irony of those dogs' names couldn't have been more evident. It seemed there were animals everywhere. An otter family had lived there once, up closer to where the creek brings in the fresh spring waters. I remember when I first learned of them.

"Watch them now, girls," Pappy whispered to my little sister, Abby, and me. "You can tell they are otters by the way they swim with their flippers, almost like a seal."

We looked, our eyes wide open to be sure we don't miss any part of this lesson of the land. We lived in Atlanta, or "the big city" as Pappy called it.

One day, I called him over, "Pappy, look! Look at that otter! His flippers are broken." As we crouched down and he unpacked his small binoculars, he sat back, letting me look too.

"No Little Nugget, that's a beaver. Dang it!" he said slapping his knee.

"Dang it!" I said, mimicking him. Then innocently, I asked, "Pappy why are we dangin' it'? Is a beaver bad?"

"Well, not to you and me particularly," he went on, "but if they get a whole family up here, they can take the timber down in a jiffy. And that is bad news, indeed bad news."

"But," I reasoned with him. "There's only one, so maybe he is just visiting." I knew what happened to unwanted critters around here. For some unknown reason, since I'd spotted him, I felt like he was mine and I wanted him to stay.

"Well, Little Nugget, since you're going home tomorrow, I'll just take the time to study up on it. If he is just a visitor, like you say, then he can visit. "

I looked up at him, "Can he really, Pappy, oh, please can he really?"

He squeezed me tight without an answer. I guess deep down I knew that he would have to rid the pond of the beavers but for that moment he lets me believe in other ways - my own fairy tale pond land with just me and Abby when I was so very young.

Now, paddling around the pond, I find myself smiling. I remembered that I'd always found this a safe place to be. Safety had been an issue. After all that had happened. Back in Atlanta. Back when I was a teenager. Back when I lost my family. Back when *The Night* happened.

~~~

Age Sixteen

It would be many years after *The Night*, living with my aunt on my mom's side. Aunt Lyn and Uncle Charles were amazing really. After *The Night* my Aunt Lyn didn't think twice. She just took me home to live with her, Uncle Charles, and my nephews, Gabe and Garrett. I didn't even think to ask if I should be sent to an orphanage. She and Uncle Charles just took me in.

Everything had been destroyed. All of the art supplies from when Mom and I used to paint were gone. I had to get all new clothes and my new bedroom was entirely different in every way, too. This house was more contemporary whereas mine had been a more traditional Williamsburg style. The ceiling here was only slightly angled, spreading longer to each side than higher. That is where, if it were my normal life, I would have put up posters up of my favorite bands and teen crushes. If I had any anymore that is. And that is where I spent many nights crying into my pillow—quietly—by myself. It was a familiar home but a new home, too. My aunt and uncle did not go unscathed either.

"Why, oh why, did they have to take my sister? And poor little Abby?" I could sometimes hear my aunt wail from behind her bedroom door.

"I know, I know," Uncle Charles would softly soothe her. But he was hurting too. The family had been close. We would go together on week long beach vacations to Sea Island; we had family picnics in our back yard with Dad working the grill and we kids running through the sprinkler; and Christmas – we always spent Christmas at their house. Yes, we had always made time to be together.

"But she is my *only* sister, I miss her, I miss her I miss her..." she would cry, trailing off. I could just picture Uncle Charles holding her in his arms, rocking her, as if she were a child, until her outburst faded.

I don't know why I didn't have another outburst. I just stopped...stopped feeling. I don't even know when that happened. The times when I could hear my aunt, I felt so sorry for her. Not for me – but for her.

Looking back, it is strange how numb I'd become. It seemed that life continued on, but it went by me like a black and white motion picture show, not really real at all.

~~~

Age Six

Abigail was born when I was six years old. When Mom came home from the hospital, I thanked them both very much and told them I would take my baby now. They laughed and laughed as I took on a consternate look. It took a bit of explaining that she was *all* of ours and that Mommy was the mommy and Daddy was the daddy and my role was to be the best big sister ever.

"The Best Big Sister Ever is a real title," my mother impressed upon me. "It requires a lot of very important tasks," she said while bobbing up and down, patting Abigail's back lightly with a pink cloth laid atop her shoulder.

"You mean like help her play dress-up?" I asked curiously.

"Oh yes!" my mother exclaimed.

"And play games?" I continued, my mind slowly thinking of how I could earn the Best Big Sister Ever Award.

"Absolutely!" Mom nodded her head in agreement, still pacing back and forth in the rhythmic cadence.

"Like peek-a-boo?" I asked, very skeptical of this smushy new little sister's ability to ever do anything.

"Well yes! But it might be a little while before she can play a lot of those games, Jenni Ann," Mom advised wisely. "She has a bit of growing to do herself."

"Well, I could sing her songs while she grows," I offered.

"Yes," laughed Mom. "You certainly could sing her songs."

I sit watching the two pass by as the wheels in my head spin.

"Can I start singing now?" I asked, ever hopeful.

"It's time to put Abigail down for a nap, so yes, let's think of a sweet lullaby for her," Mom said.

"Lullaby, and goodnight," I started singing not-so-softly, following Mom upstairs to put Abigail down for a nap.

Thinking about it after she is down and I was coloring at my playschool desk, my excitement rises. I could teach her to color. I could help her dress, play games, like peek-a-boo, and later like twister and even computer games. I could teach her all of the great songs from *Sesame Street* and *The Muppets*, and even teach her how to read. I could certainly feed her when she gets older and starts to use a baby bottle! I was satisfied with all of that. I did hope that I wouldn't ever have to change her diapers. This idea had me worrying just a bit about my title. I had just learned what real diapering is all about. It stinks! Not at all like with my baby dolls. And, I reasoned, she will be here forever. She will be with me forever. I had time. Plenty of time.

~~~

Will Hardy

Age Seven

His name was Mark. They brought him home one day as if they'd gone down the corner market for milk and bread.

"Here is your little brother," my mother said with a big smile. He was nearly two years old. He was drooling like an old hound dog and smelled funny to me. This is what my mother wanted all these years? Well, I would try to want it too.

"Hello, drooly-drooly head," I said, squinting to see if that made him look better.

"His name is Mark," my mother reminded me.

My father smacked the back of my head. "Call him Mark," he admonished me.

"Hello, Mark," I said, this time attempting to mimic my mother's enthusiasm. He smiled at me. Well, I thought. Maybe this could work out after all.

"Hello Baby Brother Mark," I said, smiling back.

"Baa daa baa daa," he gurgled back as he pulled himself up using the coffee table.

"Shouldn't he be talking already?" my mother asked my father.

"You know what they said," he reassured her. "They said it might take a bit more time due to his...um...well...environment." My father seemed uncomfortable.

"Yes, yes," my mother sighed heavily. I scampered over to her and nestled up to her on the couch.

"I like Mark and I can teach him things, too," I said, hoping to gain back that ebullient smile.

"Well yes you can William," she gaily replied. "Yes, you can."

My mother had her new baby, and, with my help, everything was going to be all right. I just knew it.

~~~

Jenni Ann

Age Sixteen

"When are they going to get that land ready for building?" Uncle Charles complained again.

"Well," Aunt Lyn consoled as we, as we cleared the dishes away from the table from dinner, "you know these things take time."

Uncle Charles turned and looked at her. "You and I both know that this is excessive politicking and it hurts the bottom line. I mean our bid did not include four months of stalling!"

"May I go to my room now?" I interjected quietly. Aunt Lyn looked over almost just noticing me. I felt invisible on the inside...was I invisible on the outside, too? Or can I really blame her? I had been keeping a distance from everyone even when we were all in the same room. I was there and I wasn't there, all at the same time.

"MOM," screamed Garrett. "Gabe won't take his bath and he's out of the tub! So can I take mine now?" Just then, a naked and soapy screaming little Gabe streaked through the room, leaving a trail of sudsy footprints in his wake.

Garrett seeing this as a perfect opportunity went flying after him. "I'm gonna get you! AHHHHHHHH!" Uncle Charles jumped up, hearing the squeals of delight, as Gabe lay hidden, undetected by his older brother, in the hall closet.

"Holy crap, Gabe, you're getting the coats all wet in here," he said as he scooped up the slippery, giggling boy and, laughing aloud, brought him back up to finish his bath. Since no one really noticed or acknowledged my request, I simply went upstairs to my new room.

~~~

The Night

It was a fairly normal streak of adolescent rebellion on *The Night.*

"NO!" my mother commands. "You will not *go to the concert at the stadium tonight. You are not old enough and I* do not *like that crowd of friends. It is a recipe for* trouble *and the answer is* no*!"*

I plead with my father, who really did try to stick up for me most of the time. Deep down, I think he was siding with Mom on this one, so I stomp out, a la *teenager, pouting with my arms flailing and all. And of course, punctuate the stomp with a swift, angry slam of my upstairs bedroom door.*

I am oblivious to Abigail who sees this as a great opportunity to paint our toenails.

"But Jenni Ann," she pleads over and over outside my door, "I've got your favorite color, Desert Green!" I turn up my music louder.

"Aw, Jenni Ann," she persists, "just because you have to stay home doesn't mean we can't have some fun....Jenni Ann?"

When she finally went to her room, I think to myself, "have some fun....are you kidding me?"

I am fifteen and everyone *is going to see the greatest band ever* – except me*! I am* missing *all of the fun! I fume and make phone calls to my friends, all of us conspiring about my life-ruining situation.*

After the evening news I hear Dad shut off the television and climb the stairs to bed. I am already missing the concert, so when he called out, "Good night Jenni. I love you!"

I reply, "Well, not so good for me, huh?"

My friends keep calling. The show was amazing—none better—they rubbed in. But hey, after party in the neighborhood. Sneak out now! It wasn't something I'd ever done before. I am not like that. But I am fifteen and I know that it is time to draw a line in the sand and show them that I am grown up! They have no right to tell me no! So I decided, Yes! I'd sneak out! I wait just long enough for the house to fall silent like it does when I'm the only one still up, usually studying. I grab my favorite crocheted beret and slip quietly down the stairs. Disarming the kitchen alarm pad, I dart out the door through the garage and into the night.

If I had only known how life-ruining my situation would become. If I had just thought of anything else but myself that night, my family might be alive today. Those words, those ridiculous, snippy words were the last I'd ever say to my Dad. All those self-centered remarks to my family, they were the last.

~~~

Age Fifteen, Summer

Our family, like so many from Atlanta, had spent the last days of summer vacationing on Sea Island. That day started the same as the last. I jumped on my bike, bathing suit cover adjusted for the trip, and headed four blocks south to Sixteenth Street to get my friend, Lizzy.

"C'mon Liz, the sun will go down before you get your makeup on at this rate," I said, exhausted with the wait.

"All right, all right," she said while giving herself a cursory last glance in the mirror. Liz was blonde, beautiful and a bit dizzy in the head. That's how she got her nickname, 'Dizzy Lizzy'. She hated it but it was a moniker that suited her.

"I mean how much make up do you *need* to go to the *beach*?"

"Hrrumph," she snorted at me. "I don't have the natural auburn beauty like you; I have to work at it, you know."

I laughed as we finally bounded down the stairs, shouting goodbyes to her parents. We cycled down the winding, single-lane path adjacent to the road, headed for the beach club.

"Do you think Adam will be there?" she called out to me from in front, the wind taking some of the words from my ears.

"Who cares?" I shouted back defiantly. I knew full well that the real question is "Do you care if Adam is there?" Of course I cared but I would never admit it out loud. Not even to my best friend.

We showed our entry cards, wrapped to our wrists in colorfully coiled rubber cuffs. Passing the main pool, we grabbed some plush white towels from the towel caddy. Looking around the main pool area all we could see were middle-aged mothers with bracelets jangling as they sipped their vodkas and old men standing around with their bellies protruding out past their toes. I lowered my sunglasses at Liz and she nodded. We knew where the fun was and it sure wasn't here. We kept going, up a set of stairs, past the Jacuzzi, until we got to the diving pool. This is where most of the teenagers hang. We scoped out two chaises, making quite a show of fluffing our towels and removing our cover-ups, finally exposing our bikini clad bodies. Yes, Adam was there, and Joey, too. Liz and Joey had been flirting for a while now and he took great notice of her arrival. Adam tried to act indifferent and I did the same. As Adam was waiting in line to climb the 10-meter board I started lotioning up my legs.

I knew he was watching and I was making a little show of it for him. Just then, the pack of mean girls passed in front of me.

"Why do you bother, Jenni Ann?" sneered The Main One. "I mean c'mon.., we *all* know *you* don't know what to do with a good-looking hunk like Adam!"

"Oh because I'm not a run around like you?" I spat back, hoping that was strong enough to get her to go away. I was not at all sure of myself.

"Oh no, we *all* know you're the total opposite of a slut, little Jenni Ann. You might as well be in kindergarten," says The Other One. Now all of them are laughing at me.

"You just shut up your nasty face and leave her alone," Lizzy is standing now, pointing her finger in the face of The Short

One. Lizzy could be dizzy but she was not a pushover; she demanded respect.

"Okay, okay. We know your both just little goody-two-shoes. Goo Goo!" says Another One as they sachet away cackling, "Goo Goo!"

I hate confrontation, especially with the mean girls.

"Those bitches," deadpans Lizzy.

"Yeah, just because I don't run around giving it away to everyone like them," I said. "Thanks Lizzy."

Deep down the exchange bothered me. Was I a goody-two-shoes? Not only did I not run around, I'd never been "around." I'd never even French kissed before.

"No need to thank me," she seethed. "I *hate* those girls."

Just then we were distracted by a loud cheering from a crowd of onlookers. One of the real tough jocks was bouncing at the end of the diving board, higher and higher each time. Then, with his hands shooting up to the sky, he leaps upwards starting what would be a great show of starting a swan dive and ending in a full gainer.

"Well that was a real quality dive, you have to admit it, Liz, right?" I asked, while she adjusted her oversized sun hat.

"Yes, indeed, Jenni, and I give him a 9.5," she said as she reached down and lifted her sign from her green and pink striped Lily Pulitzer beach bag. She displayed the score prominently, along with many other girls along the perimeter of the pool. Hooting and hollering, the boys liked the attention. We smiled at each other, liking the game as well. It was then Joey's turn on the high dive. Lizzy watched intently, biting her lip a bit. Joey was good, but not like the jocks. He chose a swan dive and this time did not end in an ego-bruising belly-flop.

"Whoo hoo!" shouted Lizzy, as Joey paddled back to the side and she marked a 9.0 score for him to see. It was a showplace at the diving pool.

It was Harvey's turn. Harvey was a great, smart, likable guy, but he had absolutely no physical attributes that would show off well in this arena. He was the funny guy and always came up with his own material.

"Go Harvey!" yelled another guy, because they liked his shtick too. We all watched to see what he had thought of today. Harvey smiled, looking around, as he grabbed an unattended pink dinosaur floatie, probably left by some six-year-old little girl, and dragged it up the ladder with him. We are already giggling, watching, waiting. We shield our eyes from the sun's glare, looking up at him, as he pulls this ridiculous pink floatie, almost impossibly, over his midsection, and bows graciously from the platform.

"Whoot, whoot, go Harvey!" screamed some of the guys, their skin sparkling with the pool water dripping off of their suntanned bodies.

Harvey then makes a show of putting on nose clips and bows yet again. This time we are all up and clapping and chanting, "Harvey...Harvey..." He makes a seriously funny face, leaps from the diving board and goes kicking and laughing the whole way down. Liz showed her scorecard with the number 10.

"Hey, Liz," I said, "you gave Joey a 9.0 and Harvey a 10? What's up?" Slapping her card down on her 50 SPF-coated legs, she exhaled loudly.

"Look, Jenni Ann, you know this is the only way he can get the girls. Let's give him a break." Looking over, I could see she was right. A small bevy of girls were waiting for him to climb up the ladder, their orange-tipped toes twirling nervously on the pool decking as they giggled.

"Yeah, I know, I know," I said as we rearranged ourselves back on the chaise lounge. And we laughed, because, really, it is very funny to see.

"Hey Lizzy," I remembered. "My parents want me to go with the whole family to Bingo tonight. Are you going?"

Liz tips her sunglasses down the perch of her nose, and, peering out from under her hat, she gives me a look.

"What?" I asked. "It's just a question."

"Of course I'm going to Bingo," she lit in. "I *love* Bingo...and *you* should go with me *every* night! Just us two and the old biddies scrambling for that elusive door prize, *every night*, Jenni Ann!" she teased.

"Okay, okay, I get your point," I said noncommittally. "But last time," I add, smiling, just knowing what her reaction will be, "they gave away a sterling silver Sea Island commemorative spoon."

"Oh, joy," she said not even looking at me this time.

"All right," I conceded. "I'll meet you at the shuffleboards after. Geesh, some friend." Which is a joke. Lizzy was my best friend, for now and as far into the future as I could see.

At Sea Island, when the parents and little ones went to bed, we kids would go out roaming the beaches, looking for sand crabs or looking for trouble. This particular night I didn't find Lizzy after Bingo. I found Adam.

"Hey, Jenni Ann," he said leaning against the railing by the shuffleboard courts. The beach breeze behind him picked up a tuft of hair, moving it back and forth across his forehead. He looked like a model out of Abercrombie & Fitch with his barely buttoned up shirt and frayed flip flops.

"Hey," I said, suddenly twisting a lock of my hair in tight ringlets with my finger. "Great diving today."

"Yea, thanks," he answered. "Say, where's your buddy Lizzy?"

"I was just looking for her," I answer, turning my face from him, scanning the courts. "We were gonna walk the beach."

"Well, I'd be honored to walk the beach with you," he says with a certain charm.

"Oh...well," I stammer. "I probably ought to wait for Lizzy."

"Ya' know," he says biting the corner of his perfectly plump lip and arching one eyebrow to the sky, "I do believe that I might have seen her headed out to the beach with some friends just a few minutes ago."

"Oh, yea?" I answer, somewhat unsure.

"Yep," he nods. "I think they went that way," he points.

I can see a group of bodies farther up the beach.

"I'd be glad to walk with you to catch up!" he offered.

I started wondering about what the Mean Girls said. Was I such a goody-two-shoes that I couldn't even walk on the beach with Adam?

"Um, well, okay. I guess," I answer.

"Great," Adam smiles, grabbing an over-sized towel from the chaise as we pass by.

"You might get cold out here with the breeze and all," he offers as an explanation.

"Umm, yea," I answer, thinking maybe now *is* the time.

As we ambled down the beach he seemed to be getting closer to me. Our arms were touching so many times he finally just takes my hand. I am blushing but thank God he can't see that.

It was all a regular kind of talk, relaxed and easy. Then, I noticed that the group that might have been Lizzy's was nowhere to be seen. They had retreated from the beach without my noticing.

"Well, maybe it wasn't her after all," says Adam, noticing, too, stopping and looking around.

"Umm...well," I am still stammering. "Maybe not."

"Let's sit here anyway," he says, laying out the fluffy white towel.

As we sit, he gets very close to me. Leaning back he reaches his arm like a strong rail touching my back, our sides joining.

"Yea, so have you ever gone skeet shooting here?" he asks as I try not to notice his closeness.

"No," I say at first, not really hearing the question. "I mean, yes! Just a little bit. Not like regularly, I mean," I say in a fluster.

"Oh, well, it's awesome," he says, turning to face me. "Really fun sport," he says leaning closer to me.

I feel my pulse quicken. The crescent moon was the perfect backdrop. Some light but not so much that Adam could actually see the fear in my eyes.

I let him kiss me, not knowing if I was doing it right, barely able to breathe. And then again. And then again. Was this the Cinderella kiss I'd been waiting for? This time Adam lifts my shirt while he's kissing me, sliding his hand up from my stomach. I feel the warm breeze.

"No," I pushed his hand down. "No, no, Adam, this is too much. This is not right."

"Aw, Jenni Ann," he smoothly crooned. "This is *so very right*. I mean c'mon baby, let me show you." He leaned into me again, his lips searing with youthful heated passion and mine wanting to answer his.

"No. No. I can't...I'm not..." I trail off knowing he wants more and me, not sure if this is the prince and if I'm in the right fairytale at all anymore!

Just then I heard the sounds of a group, giggling, spilling out on to the beach from behind us. We both turn to look, breaking away from each other. I think I hear Lizzy as they quickly get closer.

"Lizzy!" I say with relief. "There you are!"

"There I am?" she questions sarcastically. "There I am? I waited for you at the shuffleboard courts."

"Oh," I said looking back at Adam and then back at Lizzy. "Well, we thought you had already come out here," I said, wondering how his lie now became mine.

"It doesn't matter, "laughed Lizzy. "C'mon with us. We're headed up to the point to look for crabs. The tide is almost out!"

Adam and I both joined the group. He didn't hold my hand anymore that night. Or, I noticed painfully, any other night. Had I been that much of a disappointment? Was I really just a goody-two-shoes after all?

~~~

Age Sixteen, The Night

The party was fun on The Night and when I get there they are cranking some awesome tunes.

"Hey, Jenni Ann, you missed an awesome show," jeers Adam as he looks me up and down a bit too slowly for my liking. Getting closer, I can smell the beer on his breath.

"Well, maybe next time I'll be the one with the backstage passes," I counter back at him. He is tall and good-looking. A lot of girls like him. He doesn't really make great grades and this year he has been hanging out with the drinking crowd. I am not quite as impressed as I was over the summer. Before I waste another kiss on him I might just move on, I think. Just then he reaches to grab my arm and pulls me close.

"Don't waste your beer-breath on me Adam. You're not my type."

"Oh yeah," he replies, breathing directly in my face. "Well that's not what you thought last month on the beach."

"That was when I wasn't thinking at all. Now I am."

~~~

Age Sixteen, Autumn

I had no interest in concerts anymore. Or new friends at my new school. Or old friends from my old school either. Aunt Lyn was busy but she was also patient; she did not give up on her work and she did not give up on me. Every week I went to the shrink, Dr. Nancy Stewart. Dr. Stewart was okay. She was pudgy and her skirts were too long; showing only her puffy ankles and black orthopedic shoes. Her blouses tended to be oversized wildly patterned, as if the whole rainbow had spilled out of the paint can right onto her. She wore her salt and pepper hair in a bob cut. Her office was small and most of the time the receptionist was gone by the time I'd get there after school, so it would be just the two of us.

"So you *do* understand that leaving the alarm off doesn't make *you* responsible," she reiterated to me.

I nodded, thinking how full of it she was.

"Jenni, it just seems that you are putting *all* of the blame on yourself. We have been over this but I think it bears repeating," she said clearly exasperated with me. "They could have gotten in the house in any numbers of ways."

"I know that," I responded dully. "But they didn't, did they?"

I was numb. I stared at one of the cheap contemporary paintings on the wall. "Pastels," I thought to myself while she goes on and on. "Yuk."

"Jenni? Jenni? Are you listening to a thing I'm saying?" she interrupted my thoughts.

"Ahh, yeah, sure. It's not really my fault," I parroted back to her, having heard this so many times now.

"It really is that cut and dry Jenni. Really," she smiles.

I turned to look at her.

"Well then if it is so cut and dry," I said sharply, "why did the police think it best not to let that piece of information get out? Why was *it* not reported? You know why?" I asked more aggressively. "Because *it* is *why* they got in and got away with *everything*!" I jumped up and, grabbing my book bag, I ran out of the office door down the hall and out on to the street.

But Aunt Lyn wasn't coming for another twenty-five minutes, and I could hear Dr. Stewart calling out to me. I ran, skirting the front of the two-story building and ducked into the alley.

"Hey," a guy's voice calls out farther down the narrow outdoor corridor. I turned, instantly feeling like a mouse, caught on both sides by my prey.

"You're Jenni, right? From school?" called the voice.

Glancing again at him, I vaguely remember him from school. The lunchroom? The courtyard?

"Umm," I stammered, somewhat relieved that he looked harmless. As I put my finger to my pursed lips he nodded in understanding. I listened and then peeked out on to the street. Dr. Stewart had not pursued me past the front door.

I looked at the boy. He was not alone as I'd first thought but was with a girl. I recognized them both from my new school. English class? Maybe?

He waved his hand, inviting me to join them as they headed around the back corner.

"Hey, so I duuno where you are headed but I've got to wait for my Ahh...my...mom," I finished awkwardly.

"We're just going around this corner here," said the guy. Was it math class? I just couldn't place him. "It offers a bit more, shall we say, privacy."

I thought about going back to wait for Aunt Lyn on the stoop but worried Dr. Stewart would see me and make me go back in to talk to her. I never wanted to talk to her again. So, instead, I followed.

"Hey, so I can just wait here," I said wishing I knew what they needed privacy for when we were already in a back alley.

"It offers more ventilation is what he means," said the girl. "Hey, I'm Kiara."

How could I panic when she seemed so normal?

"Oh, hey," I answered, still feeling like I should turn back, like maybe this wasn't so normal after all. Ventilation? There were only a few things you needed ventilation for when you are already outdoors. "I'm Jenni."

After a turn to the left they stopped at an inset stairwell.

"So who are you running from," Kiara asked.

"Oh...um," I said glancing behind me. "I'm not running, it's just, well..."

"It's just you're hiding?" offered the boy.

"Yeah, I guess that's it. Hiding."

"And this rude one, this is Ricky," she said.

"Hi," I answered back. "I'm Jenni."

"Well Jenni," Ricky said while pulling something out of his side pocket. "How'd you like some of this?" He was grinning as he flashed a sandwich bag. Holding it from the top he let it roll down. Its contents looked a lot like Italian herbs.

Oh boy, I thought. I knew some kids from my other school that smoked pot. But I was not one of them. I was...I was...what? A goody-two-shoes?

"It's some good stuff, Jenni girl," Kiara said nodding in agreement.

"And," Ricky continued, "I've already got one rolled up!"

I pulled out my phone as a diversion, hoping that twenty-four minutes had transpired in what was actually only five minutes.

"You smoke, right?" Kiara asked looking skeptically at me.

A goody-two-shoes for what, I wondered angrily. My whole family gone, killed, because of me. Who was I being good for now? I didn't deserve goodness. Not anymore.

"Oh sure," I lied. "I've smoked before. It's just my...my mom. She's coming to get me."

I was already lying about my past, about my aunt and uncle being my mom and dad, so why not lie some more. The way I saw it, I wasn't really good anymore anyway.

"Sure," Ricky said as he lit the end of the twisted white stick. "So we won't count it against you if you have to hit and run." He sucked in deeply, holding it in.

When he passed it to Kiara, and holding it between her thumb and fingers, she did the same. Then, she offered the smoldering stick with its black ashy tip to me.

"Here," she said. "Take the joint, Jenni girl."

And I did. I put it to my lips and sucked in like they had done. I immediately was choking; blowing smoke out along with the cough that wouldn't be contained.

"I told you it was good stuff," laughed Ricky.

"Yeah," said Kiara obviously amused. "Next one don't take such a big toke."

They passed it around again and this time I took Kiara's advice. It went in my lungs. I held it. Then I exhaled. Better. I was feeling better. I wasn't thinking about Dr. Stewart. I wasn't thinking about anything.

"Yep," Ricky said. "This is some fine stuff."

I sat down on the bottom step. "Yeah," I agreed. "Fine stuff."

"So what'd you think of assembly yesterday?" asked Kiara.

"What about it?" I asked feeling fuzzy.

"Oh dude," Ricky said inhaling again. "That blowhard McMahan bitching about us being *too spirited* at the game last Friday. I mean, what does that even mean?"

"Yeah," agreed Kiara. "He's a complete waste of space."

"Oh," I said weakly. "I don't remember that part. Probably because I don't go to the football games."

"Oh dude," said Ricky. "You oughta go! We have a blast! Tell her, K!"

"Jenni, Jenni, Jenni," Kiara chided shaking her head. "You are missing the heart and soul of our entire school if you don't go to the games! I mean, then there's only...well...only school! And where's the fun in that?"

"None!" answered Ricky laughing. I don't know what was so funny but I started laughing, too! When was the last time I was with some friends...just laughing? I mean Lizzy had been calling me, but I couldn't see her anymore. Every time I thought of her, I thought about how if I'd left her that night, I'd have been home. But instead I listened, happy to be there, happy to be the one she wanted to tell her stories to. I'd have stayed out longer on *The Night* if she hadn't gone home when she did. No, I couldn't see her anymore.

We passed the joint around some more and I was forgetting Lizzy. Forgetting *The Night.* I looked down. There were ants. Hundreds of them, all lined up, marching back and forth. Bumping into one another, backing up and then realigning themselves to continue their journey. I began laughing.

"Wow," I grinned. "Look at these damn ants!"

"Whoa, dude," Ricky slowed intoned. "A resident insectologist!"

"You idiot," Kiara teased. "There is no such thing as an insectologist!"

"Well sure there is!" Ricky insisted slyly. "Our new friend Jenni here *is* one!"

Our sluggish laughter matched our goofy grins and our clouded minds.

My mind was slowing....the scene was changing. The sour scent of old urine gave way to honeysuckle vines in midsummer. The trash in the corner of the red brick building, pushed there by a light wind, became leaves fluttering on the limb of an old oak tree. Nothing could dampen this mood. It felt light and airy. Freeing. I liked it.

"Hey! Isn't your mom coming to get you?" Kiara asked looking at the time on her phone.

"Oh damn!" I said reaching for my book bag.

"Here," Kiara said pulling a piece of gum out of her bag.

"Oh, thanks," I said just noticing the green stripe indicating spearmint. I stuffed it in my mouth. "Really, thanks. Thanks for everything. I gotta go."

"Yeah," said Ricky. "See ya."

"See ya," echoed Kiara.

Coming around the corner, I could see Aunt Lyn, sitting in the car talking on her cell phone.

"Yes," she was saying as I got in. She looked over and gave me a wink. "I can show you that tomorrow. It is a beautiful old southern revival! You will love it! Yes, we're all set!"

Hanging up she looked over at me all smiles. "Well, I just might have the right buyer for the Pink Mansion! What a commission that will be!"

"Great," I answered dully. My mouth was feeling dry even with the gum.

She looked down at her phone.

"Hmm, a missed call from Dr. Stewart. So how was it today?"

"I don't ever want to go see her again," I blurted out. "I hate her and she's an idiot!"

"Whoa, Jenni Ann," she said elongating the vowels as if I were a horse needing reining in. "You hate her? What in the world?"

"She doesn't get me," I said more slowly, fishing around for that half bottle of water in my book bag. I felt my confidence soar. "She doesn't listen. And she just wants to suck you guys dry with her ridiculous fees."

"She is one of the best, Jenni Ann. That's why we pay those fees. And anyway, that is for Uncle Charles and me to deal with. "

"Well, I'm not going back."

She pushed some buttons on her phone.

"No, wait!" I stopped her. "Before you listen to her side, hear me out." I was almost slurring.

"Jenni Ann, are you okay?" she asked, eyeing me quizzically.

"I'm fine! Just tired...tired of her. I...I just can't go back to her!" I was having a hard time putting my thoughts together. I liked the way it felt when they were all scattered. I didn't *want* to get those thoughts back together. I wanted this feeling to stay with me. "So, Miss Goody-two-shoes," I thought to myself, "this is what 'good stuff' can do for you. Much better than Dr. Stewart's way."

"I'm just tired," I said again, lying back on the headrest and closing my eyes.

I could hear the faint notion of a voice on the other end of her phone as she listened to the message.

"Jesus, Jenni Ann!" she exclaimed.

I didn't answer.

"We'll talk about this later," she surmised as she put the car in gear and headed home. I slept the whole way.

~~~

Age Sixteen, The Night

Standing here on The Night, *in my friend's garage looking at Adam, I realize that saying no that night at the beach on the white fluffy towel was the smartest thing I'd done in a long time. Knowing that made it easy, too easy, to say no again, right here, back in Atlanta.*

"No thanks, I don't have time for drunk fools like you," I say, pushing away.

Just then, I see my best friend, Elizabeth.

"Lizzy!" I move over to her and we hug.

"Oh my god," she wastes no time, "you missed The Rocketeers! I am in love with Brent Bond! You know...the lead guitar player! I got a spot right up front, and, like, he played right to me I swear! Right to me!"

And on and on. She is so excited and I know she really wanted me to be there with her. I know she isn't trying to rub it in.

Next time, I think, I'd really get those backstage passes. My parents will just have to deal with it!

~~~

Will Hardy

Age Fourteen

"You're really good at this, Mark," I exclaimed, hearing the ping of a hit. We were shooting at old soda cans in the small wooded area at the end of our road.

"I wish this was what they taught in school," he replied. "Then Mom would think I'm good, too."

"Just to let you know, Mom can be real hard to please," I said. "And school, well," I winced thinking of the enormity of my brothers problems. "School can be tough for everyone," I concluded.

"I mean Mark, c'mon," I chided. "You didn't need to bust all of the beakers in the science lab. That was pretty stupid."

"Yeah," Mark said, his brown eyes looking straight ahead. "I guess so."

"So seriously what in the world made you do that anyways?" I asked while reloading the BBs.

"What does it matter?" he answered still looking ahead.

"Well, something should matter to you Mark! You can't just brush everyone off all the time! You can't just brush *me* off all the time," I said angrily.

Mark turned to look at me. It was his cold stone-hard stare that sent a shiver down my back. I dropped the tip of my gun to the ground. "Are you crazy, or what?" I blurted out before realizing what I'd said.

Mark threw down his gun and ran into the thicket.

"Mark," I called after him. I thought about chasing him. Then I thought about what I'd said.

Oh my god, I thought. *What if my brother really is crazy?*

Who should I talk to? Mom? Then I thought of all the days she spent in bed since Mark's arrival. She never talked about another baby again. Maybe the baby wasn't all she needed after all. No, not Mom. Dad?

I'd heard Dad talk to Mom about severe detachment disorder, but I didn't really know if it was Mom or Mark that had it, whatever *it* was. I was sure he'd be mad at me either way. I was stuck. Angrily I fired off all of the BBs in the chamber, making the soda can hop until it fell off the tree stump on the parched red clay.

I tried my best with Mark.

~~~

Jenni Ann

Age Sixteen, Autumn

Uncle Charles worked for a top architectural firm in Atlanta and they were busy working on a new mixed-use development in the city. It was creating quite a lot of press because it was on the site of an old steel mill, and the toxins had to be leached out before they could even start to think about putting the building he was designing on the ground. He fretted a lot about when the job would actually start and then would retreat back to his office at home to work on more drawings.

Aunt Lyn stayed so busy. She was a residential realtor and spent most of her time on the phone with clients or showing homes to prospective buyers. This meant she wasn't around a whole lot on the weekends and evenings. She was a member of the Million Dollar Club, whatever that is, and it must be good because they put an extra border around her picture in the realtors' magazines. She had studied art and architecture in college, and, as she put it, it had really paid off. Her clients were very particular, and, apparently, she was too.

Eventually, as time passed, they both seemed back in the routine, very busy with work. Between their work and the boys, that must have been what saved them. I wondered, somewhat abstractly, what would save me?

My cousins, Garrett, eight annoying years old and Gabe, six whiny years old, drove me crazy. Planes, trains, cowboys, Indians, balls, bikes. What I wouldn't have given to paint Abigail's toenails every day during those years. My memories stream through me, of holding her hand as we navigated a rocky creek bed, or of wearing our sparkly tutus and dancing and spinning together until she fell down, and we would laugh and laugh. Or of holding her in my lap, to read to her and pointing out where the mouse was hidden in the picture when she would give up. She was my sister, but at age six, when Mom and Dad brought her home from the hospital, I knew she was really my baby. *My* baby! Oh, Abigail, can you ever forgive me?

~~~

Age Sixteen, The Night

Almost home, just turning the corner, I can see the red and blue flashing lights. It can't be my house. As I get closer, the glimmer of metal on the sides of the fire trucks reflected each flash, blinding my eyes and my mind. My feet are lead. Closer. The sirens, the lights the choking black smoke. The men shouting, wearing slick yellow jackets. Weighted hoses, shooting plumes of waters. It is my house! A mix, a blur. A policeman.

"Mom! Dad! Abby!" I scream out.

The neighbor's faces don't answer.

I hear one saying to another, "The alarm, I don't know, it must not have been set."

The alarm! I panic!

"Mom!" I scream out again as I push myself forward. Only sad eyes turn to me.

"Dad! Abby!" I scream out again to anyone and everyone.

A kindly voice, a man, answers, "Do you live here?"

"Yes! Where are they!?" I look around wildly now, searching for them, thinking

maybe they are all huddled together under some borrowed blanket, having escaped.

"What is your name, miss?" the man asks calmly.

"Where is Abby? Where are they?" I keep screaming it over and over, spinning around, my eyes burning with soot.

Is it me screaming now? I don't know!

The man with the kind voice guides me away. Over to the big truck with the red light. Maybe this is where they are? Am I asking out loud? I can't hear anything. I am floating over myself. The charred smell of ashes embrace me. I am in a tunnel. Everything is far away. My senses are failing me, all but for the smell. Eventually, even that ebbs away, as if there is nothing left to see, hear, taste, touch or smell. The tunnel is longer. Narrower. Darker. I can't see anything. No sound. Fuzzy, hazy. I black out.

~~~

Age Sixteen, Autumn

In the morning at breakfast when I asked to go to Friday night's football game, Aunt Lyn and Uncle Charles were elated.

"Well, well," said Uncle Charles. "That's a change! Maybe leaving the shrink is just what you needed?"

"No." Aunt Lyn stately flatly. "That is *not* just what she needs. We talked about that last night. And she's a psychologist, not a shrink. And, Jenni Ann, you need to go see her. Going to a football game doesn't cancel out going to the doctor."

"Aunt Lyn, please don't make me. Look, how about we try it my way for a while, and if it doesn't work out, if you don't think I'm better, then I'll go back," I pleaded with her.

"No," said Uncle Charles doing a whole turnaround. "No, Jenni Ann, what your aunt says is right. You need to go." As he stuck his head in the refrigerator to pull out the cream for coffee he muttered. "And quite frankly we should all probably go."

"Yes!" I said with a tone of excitement. "Exactly! If I have to go so do you!"

"This is not a game." Aunt Lyn said. "We are getting all off subject here."

"No, I think we are all *on* subject here," I said. "If I have to go then so do you two."

At the trill of her cell phone she threw her arms up in the air and turned to answer. "Hello. Lyn Benson Realty," and stepped out of the room.

"You know Lyn will be busy showing a house on Friday afternoon, so I'll take you."

"Take me?" I questioned. The game or the shrink I wondered.

"Yes," said Uncle Charles looking up from pouring his coffee in his traveler's cup. "To the game. I'll take you to the game Friday. Now let's get going or you'll be late for school."

"Oh! Great! Thanks!" I wondered if the subject of the shrink was really over. At least it was over for now.

~~~

Age Sixteen, Friday Night

It was autumn and Daylight Saving Time made the six o'clock drop off seem even more like midnight.

"So what time do you want me to pick you up?" Uncle Charles asked.

Looking around at the throngs of people headed in the gates I had second thoughts. But Kiara and Ricky had said yesterday at school to meet them. They told me where and I'd said yes. Maybe they'd have some more pot and I could let go of myself again. The shrink wanted me to find myself. I just wanted to lose myself.

"Uh, like ten o'clock I think," I said unsurely.

"Okay, so call me if you want me to come get you earlier. We'll be out for a boys' night! Right guys?"

"Yeah," shouted Garrett from the back seat. "Boys' night!"

Followed by Gabe's, "Boys' night at the Play Zone!"

"Okay," I answered. "Have fun at Boys' night, guys!"

"Do you have enough money?" he asked before pulling away.

"I guess, sure," I answered not sure how much money one needed at a high school football game. My old school was much smaller than this one and we didn't have football.

"Here," he said pulling out his wallet. "Here's another twenty just in case. Mad money we'll call it."

"Thanks Uncle Charles," I said taking the crisp bill.

As they left the circular drive to get back off campus, I took in the enormity of the crowds and the stadium that held them all. No, my old school was just a speck compared to this, I thought. No wonder they had given me the section, row and seat numbers to find them. Without that it would have to be by total chance. I stopped and bought a bottle of water at the concession stand, remembering how dry my mouth had been last time. Last time! I thought. The *only* time! Enough of this goody-two-shoes for me! I can't possibly screw up any worse than I already have.

"Hey, Jenni," said a voice. I turned to see a girl from my English class.

"Oh, hey," I said, not knowing her name.

"Yeah, I'm Lauren. We have English together," she said introducing herself.

"Yeah, I'm Jenni," I answered. "But I guess you know that! I mean, you just said it!" I was feeling pretty stupid and wished I'd just stayed home.

"So are you meeting some friends here?" she asked.

"Um, yeah, well, I just met them, but Kiara and Ricky. I'm supposed to meet up with them." I said scanning the immediate area.

"Ewwww. Kiara Martray and Ricky Gilbert?" she asked in disgust.

"Umm, well, I guess so, I don't actually know their last names," I answered really wishing I was not having this conversation.

"Well, you can always come sit with us," she tilted her head towards a group that I recognized as being the smart kids.

"Come on, Lauren!" they yelled to her.

"Okay then, I've got to make like an amoeba and split," she said with a guffaw that showed her top front teeth.

"Okay," I answered with a little hand wave. Hopefully no one else would notice me. I was in the Atlanta city schools now, not the charter county school from before *The Night.* Anonymity was the idea when they decided to enroll me here. I wasn't known as The Girl Who Didn't Set the Alarm with these kids. No whispering behind my back about how I'd really caused the whole thing.

I looked again at the text they'd sent me. "Section CC, Row J, seats 12 to 16." I took the wide arc behind the stadium seats. When I'd climbed the stairs and reached them I realized that we were pretty high up from the field.

"Wow, this is way on up," I commented looking down below.

"Hey, Jenni," Kiara said, leaning into a guy I'd never seen before. He nodded to me as a hello.

"Jenni," said Ricky looking happy to see me. "Hey, come sit here!" He had saved a seat by him. Not that finding a seat up here would be a problem. There was just us.

I weaved through the blue plastic seats inadvertently swiveling a few as I passed.

"This is Buck," Kiara said tilting her head back in his chest as I passed in front of them.

"Hey, Buck," I said.

"Yeah, hey," he answered barely looking at me. He had on a tight black T-shirt and jeans. He had that James Dean danger look about him.

As I sat down next to Ricky I saw Buck take out a small plastic flask and turn it to his lips. He handed is to Kiara and she did the same.

"Hey," said Ricky cheerfully. "So glad you could find us!"

"Yeah, well this is one huge stadium," I remarked.

"Well, it's real easy to navigate when you know the layout. Like for instance, look out there," he said pointing across the bowl of green grass with white lines. The players' black rounded helmets moved like foosball opponents. "That side is always for the parents. Next to that, sort of mixed in, is where you see most of the teachers."

"Umm hmm," I said seeing what he was showing me.

"And then there is the sponsor section to the left of the parents. They kinda cross over some too. You can't see this from here, but they have the cushioned seats and their own concession stand. I think they serve them beer."

"I thought they didn't have alcohol at school events," I said thinking about Buck's flask.

He took another sip and laughed out loud, this time looking over at me directly. "Are you kidding me? Where did you guys find this chick?" He turned back around, offering the flask again to Kiara.

"Aww, Buck," she said. "Jenni's cool. Aren't you Jenni?"

"Oh yeah!" I said remembering how good I'd felt after meeting up with them in the alley. I wasn't a goody-two-shoes anymore. I wasn't even going to try to be a goody-one-shoe! "Yeah, I'm cool, Buck."

"Buck, dude," said Ricky. "She is so ultra-cool you can't even *tell* how cool she is!" He smiled at me and I smiled back, thankful for the endorsement.

I looked out to the scoreboard.

"Oh, we're winning," I noted after seeing the 21 Home, 7 Guests score up in lights.

"No, who is winning is Paulie and Crystal," Buck retorted.

"Paulie and Crystal?" I asked.

Yeah, well, Paulie and Crystal, ahem," Ricky explained. "They are just indisposed at the moment." He laughed along with Kiara and Buck. "In a Lover's Lane kind of way."

My mind raced. Lover's Lane? Paulie and Crystal were in our grade. Are they all "doing it"? Maybe I should put that other goody-shoe back on! But now how could I leave? I'd have to stay for a minute anyway.

"Go, team!" Kiara joked. Such a normal, sweet regular gesture. Maybe I was over reacting. Be cool, I thought to myself. Like Ricky said: I'm cool.

"Hey I brought you twenty bucks for...well...for the other day."

"Sweet," whistled Buck, not fully turning around to look at me. "A chick that brings her own dough. That is cool!"

"Aww, you don't have to," stammered Ricky.

"But I'm sure it's not cheap. And I want to," I insisted. I didn't want them cutting me out—out of the one thing that made me feel better. The one thing that eased my pain. Oh, no!

He took the twenty and shoved it in his pocket. "Hey, after security makes their sweep...which should be in..." he took out his cell checking the time. "Should be in the next ten minutes...then we can go smoke a doobie. If you want," he said looking at me.

"Yeah, sure. I want!" I answered.

Just then the plastic flask, with Buck's strong hands gripping it, were being offered to me. I'd never had a drink before. But my days as a goody-two shoes were behind me. Lizzy wasn't here to remind me. And, I reasoned, Ricky had just endorsed me as super cool.

What the hell, I thought, taking the flask. I unscrewed the shiny cap and looked down at the amber liquid. Just a sip, I thought. Just a tiny sip. I tipped it to my lips. The odor hit me before the sharp taste. I tried not to squeeze my face together too much. It was disgusting! I handed it back to Buck.

"Thanks," I said as he watched me. "What is that anyways?"

"Bourbon—straight up bourbon," he smiled and had another for himself.

Kiara checked the time. "Put that shit away Buck!" Then she handed out the gum. The same one with the green stripe on the wrapper. We all chewed our breath concealing fresheners as the rent-a-cop made his way up and around us.

"You kids playing it straight up here tonight?" he asked.

"Of course, sir. We just like the picturesque view," Ricky said. I was almost waiting for him to add "dude" at the end. He nodded and headed back down.

"What idiots," Ricky sputtered. "They come up the same time every time. How stupid do they think we are?"

"Plenty," Buck said. "That's why I'm dropping."

"Let's go," said Ricky before I could ask what exactly Buck meant by "dropping."

It was a long way down after even just that tiny sip of bourbon. Kiara stumbled a little but she just laughed.

I held the railing tightly and followed. We got to ground level and made our way to towards the middle of the stadium. Once there, we cut through a tunnel, under the seats and ended up on the outer ring on the stadium. Then, a trail took us to a gate by small stream. We could still hear everyone, but we were totally out of sight.

"Wow, this is great!" I said astonished as the remoteness while seemingly so close.

"Yep," said Ricky. "There are a few spots, but his one is probably my favorite." He lit the joint and we passed it around. Each small puff left me floating a bit higher. Not feeling...that was what it did. And I liked it again as much as the first time.

"So, Buck," started Kiara. "Hey don't drop man. You're so close!"

"I gotta," he said through his exhale. "I'm not gonna pass anyways and I've got a job lined up."

"Lined up where?" asked Kiara.

"Oh, baby," he answered with a slur. "At the motorcycle shop like I told ya'. Vroom, vroom." He lifted his hands as if shifting gears on a Harley.

"Dropping out dude," said Ricky. "Seriously that could be cool."

"At the shop?" Kiara asked in disbelief.

"It's like the existential equivalent of charting your journey, dude," Ricky philosophically surmised after his third puff.

"Yeah," said Buck pulling out his flask again. "Real cool."

We all took a sip and this time it didn't burn my throat quite as much.

"Yeah," I agreed in a smoky haze. "Real cool."

"Well, I don't think it's so cool...but whatever," Kiara said, giving in to the gentle foggy aura that surrounded us all.

"Did you hear that?" asked Kiara. There was a rustling. The joint went out and the flask was slipped back in Buck's side pocket as Ricky led us along the creek. I thought this was immensely funny and it was all I could do to keep from laughing out loud. Then we broke out into a light trot, all of us giggling. When we got back up to sandy ground behind the stadium we were all laughing and breathing hard.

"Man, I know this school better than anyone, dudes," Ricky boasted. "Just call me the Westside High School sherpa!"

I felt buoyant as we wound our way back up to our previous spot in the stands. We were all bumping into the seats and, just like little waves, they moved back to their original positions as we passed.

This was now my new group of friends. And this is what I did with them. Aunt Lyn and Uncle Charles were just so happy that I had friends. They kept offering me "mad money" and I kept spending it. Spending it like mad.

~~~

Age Sixteen, The Night

"Do you know why the alarm was not set?" *Again,* The Question. *They were treating me like a suspect. That suited me just fine because as far as I was concerned I had killed my family. And I kept saying so.*

"I killed my family! I left the alarm off! I did it! Oh, God! Take me away!" *I'd demanded.* "Or better—kill me too, kill me now!"

Detective Will Hardy, the one with the kind voice, was why they backed off. He was the lead detective. He had some years on the job and didn't need to kick around some poor teenager who just lost her family in order to get the next promotion. But I cannot see his obvious concern. I am not able to discern his caring and gentle handling of me, of his guiding me. I could not see the events unfolding, in the way he could, drawing from his years of experience. All of this escaped me entirely.

~~~

Age Sixteen, Winter

Football season ended and it was colder outside. Finding places to hang out was trickier.

"We are on the way," Kiara said over the phone. We were standing outside the back of an old church, the building itself condemned. A tired spire with an anemic cross still stood on the roof like a whisper. 'Shusssh' it said: 'Jesus was here.'

The temperature had dropped to the mid-30s and the wind was picking up. It was too cold outside, even for us.

"Alright, Ricky," Kiara directed. "You remember where Buck lives, right? Off of Buford Highway?"

"Yeah, kinda," Ricky was thinking. Sometimes, thinking was optional, so he had to work at it. Kiara was quicker and smarter.

"Get in the car. I'll tell you where to go," she finalized it for us.

"You know," I wondered aloud. "I should go ahead and get my driver's license."

"Yeah," Kiara asked from the backseat of the little black Chevy. "You are already sixteen, right?"

"Yeah," I answered. "I've got my learner's permit but I just never did go get my license." Of course, I didn't. After *The Night* nothing has been the same. Why should it?

"Whoa!" Kiara shouted from the back at Ricky. "*No*! Don't turn here!"

"Relax, K," he assured in his strawberry smoothie voice. "It looks like Johnny's working the counter here and I've got a little pick up to do." A light green VW beetle bug was the only car to be seen and was parked to the side of the quick-mart.

"Mmmkay," she nodded.

I opened my door, stepping out to join Ricky.

"No, baby," he said. He came over to me and leaned me against the car door. "This is one the Rickster has to do by himself." He gave me a quick peck on the lips.

"Okay, baby," I complied.

Back in the car with Kiara, I was curious.

"He's getting beer right? K?"I turned to her.

"Honey, whatever he's getting we are gonna be happy about it, so don't you worry," she reassured me.

"So," she continued. "You and Ricky are getting along pretty well, huh?"

"Yeah," I answered blushing a little. "I really feel great with him." I turned to look at him through the window. It all looked like a normal transaction from here. "Really great..." I trailed off.

"Well," she advised. "Just make sure you use condoms. You don't want a baby daddy!" she snickered and we gave each other a high five.

"What about you and Buck?" I asked. "Is it serious?"

Oh," she answered vaguely. "Is anything ever serious with Buck? I mean he dropped out of school to work in the motorcycle shop. I wonder about him. But I love him...yeah, so, I'd say it's serious."

The vacuum seal of the driver's door was broken, interrupting us.

"Ooh la, la," Ricky crooned dropping a bag with a twelve-pack of beer in the seat. "We are gonna have some fun tonight!"

Ricky's parents had money, so he had money. And he had the car. It made him the unofficial Leader. Kiara was the Brains. Buck was the Brawn. So what, I wondered, was I? I looked over at Ricky and smiled. Before he backed out, I leaned over and gave him a kiss. A real kiss. The Lover, I thought. I'll be the Lover. No one in this group knows about my awkward preteen years. About my goody-two-shoes reputation.

"What kind of fun?" I asked in anticipation.

"The White Horse has ridden in to town," Ricky said as if at a poetry reading in a Little Five Points coffee shop.

"Ohh, yeah!" Kiara cheered. "Sweeett score, Rickster!"

"*White Horse*?" I shook my head not understanding.

"The powder of the gods, my Jenni dudette," Ricky said, steering the car into a shabby apartment complex. There were signs of shrubbery past held back by broken cement curbs. Jagged pavement fronted up to the peeling brick, two-story units. Buck's motorcycle was a shiny toy next to an old huge rusty Buick.

"Damn it's cold out Buck!" Ricky said as he entered. "Why'd you make us wait so long?"

Buck reached out to Kiara and pulled her in for a kiss.

"Ricky, you know I gotta work now," Buck answered between kisses. "And I've missed my Baby K!" He was freshly showered and smelled like Irish Spring soap.

"Who wants a brew?" Ricky called out from the kitchen over the sound of aluminum sliding on metal refrigerator racks. "Oh! And, Buck! Do I have a surprise for *you*!"

Ricky chose the tacky big brown chair. He pulled the table a bit closer to start crafting this surprise. I watched as he took out a plastic baggie with white powder. He deftly poured some into a paper, added the pot, and rolled it all together. He made four in all until the white powder was gone.

"The White Horse is *here*!" he announced triumphantly as he lit the first joint.

It wasn't long before I was in the chair with Ricky. I didn't even notice when Kiara and Buck moved to the bedroom. I was sitting on his lap, kissing him. He was kissing me. We were falling from the sky. We were floating. We were laughing and touching. Lips...slowly...moving. Lips touching lips. And our hands were the branches of our centers, reaching out, wanting to know more. Wanting to reach the sensation of that sun inspired blossoming. It was all was so warm, so ingeniously planned in the universe. No questioning. No protesting. No other way in the world that was more right then in that moment. I was the *one*, the one who deserved this love and weightlessness from my Knight in Shining Armor. My Prince who came to me on his White Horse. I was rocking my internal lullaby with his every touch. This was where I was meant to be. Nothing else mattered. Nothing.

~~~

Age Twelve

"Mom, that's really good!" I exclaimed admiring her canvas. I was twelve and Abby was six. We were in the basement in what I called the Art Studio. It was a small room with two windows flanking an outside door. There was a small bathroom with a sink full of old paintbrushes, most just dried out until they were useless and we needed to go get more again.

On the walls hung some sketches in pencil and some watercolors too. The linoleum floors were speckled with color. On this day we were learning about the oils.

"It's okay, I guess," she answered with a grimace of her lip. "I haven't touched the oils in a while. I'm a bit rusty."

The scene was from the zoo where she had taken Abby and me that past weekend. It was the new panda from China. The bamboo shoots were green leafy bits hanging from her lips as she was mid-chew. Her eyes were sloped inward, begging you to furrow your brow with her and contemplate the apparent problem.

"No, Mom," I insisted. "It's really good! I mean look how you captured her sad eyes."

We both moved closer to scrutinize the painted face.

Abby was painting what look like a glob of yellow. She insisted it was the lions.

"Roar, roar," she would playfully act out while she globbed on more yellow and then smeared it together with her hands.

Mom had painted before, in her youth. I found myself impressed with her talent.

"Mom," I asked. "Why did you stop?'

"Hmmm," she looked over at me distractedly

"Why did you stop—stop painting?"

"Jenni Ann," she said, "I moved down here and had you and your sister. The most two precious gifts from God ever given to me, and simply didn't need to anymore."

Now Abby had the blue and was sliding it in an arc across the top of her paper.

"What is the blue Abby?" Mom asked with interest.

"It's the skyyyyyyyyyy," she sang out with glee.

"Pappy said you used to paint a lot," I interjected. "He said you wouldn't paint anymore after you were sixteen. He said you *couldn't*, that you just stopped."

All of a sudden her eyes took on the sadness of her panda.

"Pappy said all that, huh?"

"Yes, he told me you were good though." Looking over at her panda was proof. "And he was right, Mom. He was right."

"Well, I just grew up is all. Sometimes things happen in life and you just have to accept it and grow up. And really this painting is more your area, Jenni Ann. I'm just playing."

With that she put her brush down.

"Come here you little, Abby Mess," she said holding out her hand for Abby who was thoroughly covered in yellow and blue paint. "Let's get you cleaned up!"

"But Mom," I pleaded. "This is so good!"

She went to the shower and did the preliminary wash off, removed Abby's little jumper and left it on the shower stall floor before wrapping her up in a towel.

"Why would you stop?" I persisted.

"Not now Jenni Ann," she replied. Then she turned her attention back to Abby.

"We need to get you in a proper bath," she said circling her finger at Abby's belly.

"Wheeeee," Abby squealed at the spiraling tickle that had not even touched her at all. Mom swung her around as she scooped her up and they went upstairs giggling and squealing.

I do not ever recall another time when I saw Mom pick up a paintbrush.

~~~

Age Sixteen, Early June

As summer's heat scorched the blacktop under my thin-soled sandals, we made our way back to the car.

"Oh, wow," I exhaled now that we were out of the building. "I can't believe I just passed my driver's test! I've got my license!" I said waving the flimsy paper license that would soon be replaced by a laminated one sent in the mail from the good State of Georgia.

"Let's go get me a car!" I said excitedly.

"Now, Jenni Ann," Aunt Lyn began, "you know the insurance money is first and foremost for your education! We will have to save up just a little to get you a car, hon."

"Well, yeah," I said, still not dissuaded. "I know, but we could go looking, you know! Oh!" I stopped just short of the car. "Can I drive us home?"

"Jenni Ann," she sighed as she opened the driver's side door and slid in the seat. "Get in. We need to talk."

As I walked around to the passenger side I muttered, "Ohhh-kaaay."

What? Talk? I just got my license! This did *not* sound good.

"Jenni Ann, your uncle and I have been worried about you," she said, pulling out on to the four-lane highway.

It seems she did her best talking in the car.

"About what?" I asked in disbelief.

"Honey, your grades really dropped this year." Silence. "All of them."

"Well, I didn't actually fail anything. And anyways it's just me getting used to the new school and all," I reasoned with her as I ran my thumb down the gray paper proudly showing my achievement. Why was she bringing this up now? The ink was just drying.

"No, Jenni Ann, it is not. You've been there long enough and you've made friends. It's just, well, we think maybe you should make more friends. Some other friends."

"What's wrong with my friends?" I asked. I had never thought about whether she and Uncle Charles actually liked them. Of course she doesn't like them! If she only knew the whole of it! There was not even a glint of defiance in my voice.

"Your uncle and I, well, we just feel that you could do better. You barely hang out with us at home and when you do you sleep. Your grades went down and you seem a bit, um, detached. And with Ricky, I mean, is he your boyfriend now?"

"Yeah," I said, wishing I were with him. But he had to go on his family vacation and would be gone for a week.

"Are you having sex?" she asked. Just like that.

"Aunt Lyn," I exclaimed. "Of course not! How could you think that?" When had I gotten so good at lying? Why did it crush me each time?

"Jenni Ann, how could I *not* think that?" she retorted. "The *last* thing I want is for you to end up pregnant and with a flake like him!"

"A flake," I cried out. "He is the smartest, sweetest guy ever!" I said in his defense.

"Honey, really," she said more evenly now. "You really need to go back to Dr. Stewart. She can help."

"But I don't *need* help," I protested.

"Jenni Ann, you don't paint at all anymore and I bought you that beautiful new easel and paints. What's really going on? Hmm?"

As the tears rolled down my face I was trying to answer that too. I thought what was going on was that I had good friends and a boyfriend and I wasn't so angry anymore. I was feeling good! Wasn't I? Is that what I was feeling? If I had to say it out loud, it would be that they were a bunch of pot-smoking druggies who were having sex. Is that what I'd become too? Merely that, and nothing more? Where was my mommy now? Now, when I *needed* her?! What had she said? She said that sometimes things happen in life and you just have to accept it and grow up. Accept it and grow *up*! Isn't that what I was doing?

Not another word passed between us until we turned on our street.

"Hon," Aunt Lyn spoke softly. "We'll talk more about this later. In the meantime I promised the boys some ice cream. Maybe you could drive us all to the ice cream shop?"

It was a peace offering. We never talked about anything "later." Her feelings were out there and now I knew. That would be all.

"Yeah," I said collecting myself for the rolling tumbleweed that was Garrett and Gabe; always going somewhere and never in a straight line.

There they were on the front lawn throwing a ball and jumping all over each other.

"Yeah, that'd be great," I finished with a smile hiding the dark clouds in my head.

~~~

Age Sixteen, Late June

"But Kiara, if you want to borrow these shoes for your trip she'll let me drive over there!" I explained through the phone.

I flopped down on the bed belly first and hung my head to look underneath for the shoe's mate.

"Are they the ones with the crisscross top and the strappy thing?" she asked.

"Sure," I answered wondering if we were talking about the same shoes at all.

"But see, the shoes are not the point here," I explained.

"Well okay then I get that," Kiara said sarcastically. She was the smart one. She had goals. She did well in school. She wasn't just a pothead. I was sure of it!

"Look! Got 'em! I'll see you in fifteen minutes!" I hung up quickly.

Ricky wouldn't be back for three more days. He was going to go to college for sure because he did okay in school. He'd talked about it! He wasn't just a druggie! My friends were real and I was certain of it!

With Kiara leaving for a whole week, I just *had* to see her. How could I make it without my friends?

"Aunt Lyn, Kiara needs to borrow my shoes. They are leaving and she needs them now," I said while dangling the car keys in the air. "Can I?"

"The question is 'May I' and the answer is yes," she said. "But please be back at a reasonable time."

"Of course," I smiled and gave Uncle Charles a peck on the cheek. "Absolutely," I said again, as if to gain more of their confidence.

The blue Volvo wagon wasn't exactly the hottest car to be seen in, but it got me there. They were packing luggage on the top rack of the minivan as I pulled up.

"Hello, Mr. Martray," I said politely to her father.

He grunted something while hanging off the top with ropes in his teeth.

Kiara ran out and pulled me inside and upstairs to her room.

"I'm gonna miss you, girl," she said throwing her arms around me.

"What am I gonna do without you? And Ricky too?" I whined. "Can I fit in your suitcase?"

"You're the funny one!" she laughed.

Her mother was calling from the hallway. It was time for her to go.

"I'll miss you," I said again as we trotted down the steps to the driveway.

"One last hug," she said. And then they drove away. I waved until they turned the corner.

I was alone again. I was afraid. I needed to score some stuff or I'd never feel better. Buck? I'd never been over there with just Buck. I pulled out my cell.

No, I thought. Don't call. If I call and he says no then I can't go over. But if I go over and he's there then I can just sort of stop by.

It turns out he was glad to see me. He had just scored and was more than happy to share with me. Then, he popped open a small plastic bottle and poured some pills on the table.

"You'll love it, Jen," he said slowly. It makes you feel calm and smooth and free," he said as he sailed his hand across the imaginary glass-topped sea.

"But what is it? What does it do?" I asked, not feeling entirely comfortable.

"It makes you happy, Jen! Happy!" he grinned over at me.

"Here," he chuckled as he threw a bag to me. "Roll one up then. But you'll be lovin' this happy pill more than anything, I promise!"

In my fervor to get a joint rolled I didn't notice the way Buck was looking at me. I missed it when he went to be sure the door was locked and the blinds drawn. I was too eager. I wanted the feeling. I needed to escape. Earlier, standing alone in Kiara's driveway waving goodbye, it felt like an end.

Buck popped a pill in his mouth. Smiling, he gestured for me to pick one and take it. Where was Buck going in life? He quit school and worked at a motorcycle repair shop. He dreamed of owning his own shop one day. That was ambition, right? He wasn't just a loser; no, he was a winner! And so I grabbed his beer can and put the pill in my mouth, swallowing it down with a big gulp.

"You know," I spoke out. "I always feel so good around you guys."

"What guys," Buck said slowly looking around the room.

"Oh, you know," I said taking another toke. The effects were exactly what I needed. Finally feeling good again!

"Ricky and Kiara and us and all," I was smiling. "Hey, what'd I take anyways?"

"If you take it and don't ask then maybe you should see how you feel and *you* tell *me* what you took," he said jokingly.

"No, really," I laughed.

"No, really," he laughed back.

Was he talking slower? Or was I hearing slower? The music was coming in and out of my ears in waves. What were we listening to?

"Wow!" I said. The sound of my own voice was like a hollow tin drum.

"Is this acid or LSD or something?" I asked, not quite sure if what I'd said came out the same way.

"Ecstasy, Baby," he said.

I was fascinated with his lips. They were moving extremely slowly. I got closer. I sat on the couch touching his lips with my hands. He took my hands away and pulled me to him. I don't even know where the real and the not-real crossed over. I had no sense of time passing. I had no thoughts of Ricky or

Kiara. It was just me and Buck and our bodies, together. Time had no measure and the lightness outside made way to darkness without my knowing.

The next thing I remember is the pounding on the door.

"Jennifer Ann! Jennifer *Ann*!"

I looked around in confusion. A few slits of daylight streaked through the broken metal blinds. My head felt like a ten-pound weight.

"Oh God!" I said shakily. I was in bed totally naked, with Buck!

"*Jennifer Ann*, you open this door or I'm calling the police!" I could hear Uncle Charles shout.

At the word "police" Buck sat right up.

"What the hell?" he looked over at me. "Hey if you're gonna cause me trouble with the police then get the hell outta here," he snarled.

"Buck," I stammered. "I don't know. I'm not sure."

Bam, bam, bam on the door.

"Just call the police, Charles," I could hear Aunt Lyn saying.

"Get out!" Buck yelled.

The confusion was overwhelming. Why was he yelling at me? I thought he loved me now? Where were my clothes?

"I said *get out*, Bitch!" he yelled again. "I'm not going to jail for you!"

Stumbling over his shoes, I grabbed my shorts, pulling them on. Where was my underwear? It was so jumbled! I reached frantically at a T-shirt. His? Mine? I yanked it over my head. I felt like dirt. Did I really sleep with him? Oh God, my aunt and uncle! I have the car! I didn't go home! The heft of my handbag landed at my feet where Buck threw it.

"I said get out!" he hissed.

Opening the door and falling out into the bright light and hot anger was no better than inside. I felt like dirt on top of dirt.

"I'm sorry. I'm so sorry," was all I could muster up. "I'm so, so sorry." I wanted to go back in time. I wanted my mommy. I wanted her to hold me and tell me it would all be all right now, like when I was little. "I'm so sorry," I said again falling into the back seat of the car.

"Do you have *any* idea how worried we were? Look at you! You're a stinking mess!" Uncle Charles was yelling at me now too. Dirt on top of dirt covered with dirt.

"Let's get home," Aunt Lyn said disgustedly. The neighbors were opening front doors and peeking out of window blinds.

I felt my insides turning out. I grabbed the door handle and with no grace whatsoever, let my retch spill out on to the pavement.

Aunt Lyn jumped into the back of the car and pulled me back in when I'd stopped. She pulled out a carry bag and handed it to me.

"Use this if you need to on the way home."

"Lyn," Uncle Charles said sternly, "take the other car. Let's get the hell out of here."

~~~

The day after they pulled me out of Buck's apartment they both escorted me without ceremony to Dr. Stewart's office. Aunt Lyn was clear. I had no choice.

"An in-house facility? You mean a mental ward!?!" I was shocked. "Oh, no, I don't think so, no not at all."

"More like a rehabilitation center," interjected Dr. Stewart.

"You are a drug addict, Jenni Ann. You told me yesterday that you didn't even know *what* you were taking it and you just *took* it," Aunt Lyn was almost frantic. "You took it with that, that—guy! And who is *he*?"

I wanted to say he was a friend. But now I wasn't sure what he was—or what I was. I thought all of these pills and the pot would make it all go away! What was happening?

Aunt Lyn looked over at me, her face clearly worn from the worrying.

"You have a serious problem, Jenni Ann," Uncle Charles said sternly. "We are only trying to help."

"What the hell?" I stammered. The attacks were coming from all sides. "What the hell would you all know about my 'serious problem'?"

"More than you think, Jenni Ann," started the doctor.

"And *you*!" I lashed out at her. "You don't have the *right* to call me Jenni Ann!" I stood up pointing at her. You're not my *family*!" Suddenly my breath became shallow. The word 'family" was too much for me to hear myself say out loud.

"Jenni Ann," Aunt Lyn exclaimed standing up, gripping my arms. Looking at her, eye to eye, I broke down in tears.

"My family," I cried, falling like a baby in Aunt Lyn's waiting arms. "My family!"

The room was quiet. I don't know how many minutes passed before I stopped sobbing and lifted my head.

"What you're doing isn't bringing them back, Jenni Baby," Aunt Lyn said as she stroked my hair. "*We* are your family and we love you. We *won't* lose you this way. You hear me?" she finished softly.

"Jenni," said Dr. Stewart. "I know this much. You have had a tremendous tragedy. You've been entirely uprooted. You have to know that in order to make your life better, we have to get you straight first. Then, we'll go over some ways to help you cope. Ways to help you live. Ways to be happy again. The way you've been going—it does not have to be your life."

My life? Was this is my life?

I nodded my head. What would Mom and Dad think of me now? How would Abby ever look up to me when I am like this? My Life? No, no, no! All the drugs were swirling in my system. But this was not who I was in my heart. I needed out!

I looked at Dr. Stewart through panda bear eyes. Barely whispering, I begged, "Help me."

~~~

Age Sixteen, The Night

The two men are intent on their mission. They see me. They see how I make my exit and leave the alarm turned off. Now they know that they can jimmy the door easily. They can do the job tonight. There will be no warning. And there would be more time. More time to get the job done. They bust open the master bedroom door and bam-bam-bam shoot my father dead as he lay in bed, sleeping beside my mother. There is no forewarning from the house alarm, no time for my dad to reach in the bedside drawer and get the .38 revolver, loaded and unlocked for just this kind of situation. The two men then pull my mother out of bed, blood splattered on her face from the first three shots. They grab her and shove her against the wall so hard her head lolls momentarily to the side. Jerking her up again, they make her get all of the jewelry and money. How can I know that she begs, "Please, no, please!" before bam-bam, two more shots killing her dead.

~~~

Age Sixteen, Late August

The days were the same. They never wavered. In the rehab facility, routine was the routine. The abrasive beginnings with the others gave way, as our barriers were broken down, to an environment of broken fragile figures. All of us slowly rebuilding and reuniting with our unresolved selves. Art therapy was my comfort. It is there that I felt most at ease. This is where I could bear my soul. Find my heart. Exorcise my pain. Let it out.

The doctors and counselors preached that these people would be my forever friends. I knew that was not true. Not for me. I saw a bigger, brighter future. I painted it over and over. The flames of redemption were blazing up from every scene. Even the tranquil stream in winter held a small corner, a glance of a sunrise, beaming with fire, over the hillside. It was my ray of hope. It was my true self. Learning to cope with my tragic past, yet knowing, presciently, that there was more...more for me...more yet to come. It was an internal unspoken mantra – humming in my spirit – coming out on my canvas as if in a trance.

The day came when Aunt Lyn and Uncle Charles took me home.

"We are going to see Dr. Stewart tomorrow," said Aunt Lyn. "And we will get you back in school. Something small, but lovely." Her words tumbled out without pause. She seemed more nervous than all of us after my six weeks away.

"Unless you're not ready Jenni Ann," Uncle Charles abruptly added.

"I'm ready," I smiled. "I am sure I'm ready."

Watching the scenery change from the flat, parched South Georgia to the green grasses as we moved north, I knew I was ready.

~~~

Age Sixteen, Late August

"Hi, Lyn, Charles, Jenni," greeted Dr. Stewart. She sat at her antique roll-top desk, the papers piled in uneven forms around a large laptop computer and called to us from the open door. "I'll be right with you; please have a seat."

The pastel prints on the wall were still as bland as the rosy course woven couch. Dried hydrangeas sat in a low round vase, maintaining their blue even as the dust accumulated atop their blooms.

This time, sitting in the waiting area, I felt sadder than before. They had explained some of this to me at the rehab center. I had to use my anger to heal. It was only a result of my sadness. My grief. I had to talk. I had to find my outlet—a safe outlet. My mind was my own again after the thirty days. I'd regained my mind. Now I had to regain my soul.

"So you see," the doctor explained once inside with the door closed, "it is a family dynamic that requires something of everyone. It's not just Jenni who has to do the work."

"Well, yes, but you see, now, I can spend more time with her. I've just finished with a complicated listing and I am not taking any more listings for a while. I can spend *a lot* more time with Jenni. And, well, we can work this out," Aunt Lyn stammered, looking to me. She wore her guilt like a coat of arms for all to see.

"That is good, Lyn," she encouraged. "I think this whole family needs to work this out. And I know you can."

"Well," Uncle Charles jumped in, "we are doing what we think, er, or, what we thought was best for her." His mind was calculating his errors.

"You know, Mom was one hundred percent against drugs," I said reluctantly. Mom and I had had the talk many times, about how drugs can make you feel good at first, or else people wouldn't keep taking them, and then, you could get stuck, hooked, and not find your real self again.

"You remember how Mom would say that a perfectly fabulous, intelligent, empathetic person can turn into a ghastly shell and their whole life can be ruined? I knew better.

Please don't feel so bad." I said glumly, adding my shame to our list of infractions.

"If I can't ever have Mom back at least I can honor what she taught me when she was here," I whimpered. "I miss her so much all the time and I don't want to do drugs."

"Yes. So let's start by getting you enlisted in a small private school. It is imperative that you get out of that environment at the city school."

Aunt Lyn and Uncle Charles took the paper she handed them.

"You mentioned Jenni has enjoyed art in the past," Dr. Stewart said. "I recommend the one I've starred, here," she leaned over pointing with her pen. "They have excellent resources and a first class arts department."

There I was, a passenger. I had proven I couldn't be in charge of myself, so I let it happen. But then, I could see my uncle's eyebrows rise with concern.

He let out a small whistle.

"Okay, but what being able to afford it?" he leaned over to consult with Dr. Stewart.

"Well they all have financial aid," she said sitting back in her seat. "As I noted, the one for Jenni is the Huff School for the Arts. It is geared to empower young people through the arts. And of course it is a fully accredited school as well."

No one spoke.

"And continue to see me weekly," Dr. Stewart said smiling.

"They've just started about ten days ago," she added as we were leaving. "She's a smart girl, so she won't be too far behind."

~~~

Age Seventeen

I could hear the phone ring, once, twice, three times. I didn't want to answer so I laid there and waited for the sound of the answering machine.

Hello, this is the Benson family. We can't get to the phone right now, so at the sound of the tone, please leave a message. *Beeep.*

"Umm, hey, Jenni Ann. It's Lizzy again. I just was headed to the senior class pep rally and thought of you. Like I always do. So I guess you changed your cell phone number again, 'cause I get some guy from

Ohio when I call. Ha! Well, I miss you. Um, well, hmm okay then...bye." Lying in my bed, I stared at the slanted ceiling listening to her voice. I missed her too. Or maybe what I missed was my life. The trajectory of my life like it was before. I'll just never feel like the girl I was back then. Lizzy could never understand. I was seventeen. It was my senior year. I was alone.

~~~

Pottery. Pottery is what Dr. Waters introduced to the class. Some had great skills and a few, like me, did not. The process was totally foreign to me. Cut the clay off the block, get your damp sponge, the pushing, pulling, prodding, protruding; this was so gross.

Dr. Waters could see how out of place all of this was for me.

"Jenni, how is your project going?" he asked one day.

"There is too much slime and where is the color?" I responded.

Dr. Waters explained to me how the color is put on after and then fired in the kiln later.

"You see," he pontificated loudly for the whole class to hear, "the glazing process and the firing technique affect the finished product as much as the building, or throwing process."

I was glad when he continued his walk around the class. Let him make a speech to another student.

Although I did not really like the clay, I still found myself looking forward to art class. Dr. Waters was gentle and it felt safe in that room. Sometimes I would come after school and work alone. I could hear the coach's yelling to the players practicing in the field below the building. And I could hear the clashing of lacrosse sticks as they crashed into each other, violent and sudden.

This energy somehow drifted up from the field, through the window, and came to me. Soon I found myself working hard with the clay, kneading and pulling it as if it were a stubborn weed showing itself in the garden at the old homeplace. Then, beating the clay, harder, like the punches of a wild child, having no desire to stop, my anger intent on destruction. Destruction of *The Night*, the destruction of my secret. My anger didn't produce anything you would call a piece of art during that semester. Instead, something scary started happening to me. I started to feel again. It was anger. And it was more. It was a feeling from deep down inside of me.

After fighting so many of those demons in that classroom, my attitude at home got a little better. I even enjoyed watching Garrett and Gabe play baseball.

~~~

Will Hardy

Age Eighteen

I never understood Mark. In one of his rages he destroyed a chair in class and proceeded to throw it right out the window. He didn't seem to care. And he didn't confide in me anymore. My mother was in need of help but not the kind that I knew how to give her. My father worked most of the time – at least that's what he told us. I know, more than once, he came home with bourbon on his breath. He was angry with his lot in life. And I was angry, too.

I took my anger out shooting my guns. It was as if I could control the world with one tiny squeeze of my finger. It begged for respect. It was as if the power of the gun strengthened me. I saved up enough to go to the shooting range. It was there that I met him. I noticed his crisp blue uniform with a patch on his sleeve outlined in gold identifying him as a policeman. He had a badge, shiny and gold, pinned to his left shirt pocket. His brown skin grew taut on his arms as he took aim and fired downrange at the target. He was an excellent shot! His gun was mighty! It exploded out of the barrel with a near-deafening boom! He laid his weapon down on the console and looked over at me. He frowned and tapped his headphones. No wonder it was so loud! I'd forgotten to put on my headphones! I quickly put them on and went to my alley. I had my .22 caliber revolver that I'd had to work overtime at the grocery as a stock boy at night to afford. Everything was muffled with the headphones on so that even the sound of loading my bullets was foreign to me. I tipped the lever to get my target to appear. I moved it up and then back again. No target.

"Did you forget something," a strong mans voice asked. I looked up and saw the policeman.

"Well, I was just trying to get my target to come up is all," I screamed so he could hear me through our headphones.

He put his hand up indicating that I didn't need to scream so loudly with a laugh.

"Ever been in a shooting range before, son?" he asked with raised eyebrows.

"Well, umm...actually, no,' I admitted. "No sir."

"You either bring your own targets or buy them here," he explained with a tip of his thumb directing my eyes to the front counter through the bulletproof glass separating us.

"Oh!" I said, wishing I'd realized that before spending my last dollar on range time.

"You can have one of mine," he said handing me a silhouette of a human torso.

"Sir," I admitted. "I can't. I don't have any more money."

"Well, this one's on me then," he said, feeling sorry for me.

"Thank you sir," I stumbled over my words. "I will pay you back next week, I promise!"

When my bullets were exhausted he examined my target with me.

"Not bad," he remarked. "Not bad at all."

"Thank you sir," I grinned. A compliment from a man in power, from a man in control. I was emboldened!

"So how much do I owe you and where can I go to pay you back?" I asked.

"No money. Just you. Next week. Right here," he said.

"Yessir! Right here! Next week! I'll be here!" I shook his hand.

And so began a career without me even knowing.

~~~

Jenni Ann

Age Seventeen

It was my last semester of high school and Dr. Waters continued our study of oil on canvas. Holding the wooden handle with the silky brush tips, dipping it in deep red, like berry jam, then into the bold white and egg-yolk yellow. The colors spoke to me. The greens were the pastures where happier times had once been. The browns were the man with the kind voice in the cheap brown suit. The oranges and reds were the flashing lights mixing with the fiery house up in flames. The yellows...yes the yellows. They were the silky tresses of my sweet little Abby's hair.

The more I learned and experimented the more I could see an image in my head. I could see what it looked like on the canvas before I even painted it all. Sometimes I would surprise myself, adding a tiny bluebird in the midst of a grove of green broad-leafed oak trees. Just to see its frailty against the mighty oaks was so powerful. I wondered if I was that tiny bluebird or that mighty oak. Guiding my brush, sliding and daubing it on the canvas—this became my passion.

"That is quite good, Jenni Ann. Really quite good!" Dr. Waters commented more than once. On one such occasion, he inquired, "Have you any ideas about where you'll be going to college?"

"College, umm, no, sir, I really haven't thought much about that," I muttered distractedly.

"Jenni, you're a senior. And you are immensely talented. I'd like to talk with your parents about SCAD."

I looked up at him quizzically.

I had taken my aunt and uncle's after *The Night*. I had been Jennifer Ann G. Cagle. Someone made a mistake at the hospital and added the "G" in my middle name. If you say my whole name aloud it sounds like "Jennifer Angie Cagle." Mom and I used to laugh at that. She always said that the "Ann" is like her middle name and the "G" is for her given last name, Gold. She said it was meant to be, so she never changed it. But now, after *The Night*, now it is different. Now it is Jennifer Ann G. Benson. And now I call them my parents. It seemed easier at the time. We just swept it all, *The Night* and my secret, right under the rug.

"SCAD," he repeated. I looked at him, mystified.

"Savannah College of Art and Design," he explained.

As it turned out, Aunt Lyn liked the idea of Savannah College of Art and Design, right here in Atlanta. I am sure she still didn't want me far away, just in case the shrink was right, and I tried to jump or something. I just know I wanted to paint.

~~~

Age Ten

Abigail, my sweet sweet Abby-Goose. I made up that nickname for her early on. She did the silliest, cutest things. Like one time she lined up all of these gemstones—agate, amethyst, rose quartz, granite, tiger's eye, greystone—and proceeded to send them two-by-two down the aisle to be married. Her blonde tendrils bobbing, she would sing, "Here comes the bride, all dressed in white."

"Oh you, Silly Goose. You Silly Abby-Goose!" I laughed back at her. She was only four years old but smart. She was much smarter than me. I would play teacher and she would be the student.

"Red. R-E-D!" she would announce, reading from her plush book.

And I would answer," Yes, Abby! Good Girl!" And then, pointing at the next page, I would ask, "And what about that one?"

"Blue! B–L-U-E," she would announce proudly, knowing she was right. Those were easy for her and it wasn't long before we'd moved on to bigger words.

And she was so pretty! I remember one of many strangers stopping us to compliment her beauty.

"Well, she is prettier than a spring day in Versailles!" came the comment one day.

"What is a vear's eye?" I asked my mother, when the lady had strolled further down the aisle.

"Versailles," my mother corrected. "It is the most beautiful estate in France! The architecture, the artwork, the gardens—and it is unequalled in its beauty, especially in the springtime!" she said. My mother loved springtime and yes, I'd thought—Abby is as pretty as Versailles! She had the emerald green eyes, the creamy white complexion and the golden yellow tresses. My Sweet Abby.

~~~

Age Seventeen

When we went for the tour of SCAD I was in heaven! *Yes!* This is where I belonged! Dr. Waters had been so right.

"Yes, she is *so much* better," Aunt Lyn reported with relief at our meeting with Dr. Stewart.

"Well, I see here she is making progress," commented Dr. Stewart, scanning some school documents.

"Dr. Stewart, I really am better. I don't need the drugs," I assured her. "I need the oils. The oils and the canvas."

"Jenni, it's not that easy," she said skeptically.

"Oh, but I think it is!" I went on to tell her SCAD was teaching me in pencil and charcoal, watercolor, etching and even mixed media.

"The encaustic techniques are way beyond anything I'd ever thought of," I continued in earnest. "But I always gravitate back to the oils."

"You have not fully dealt with some of your issues and I worry about what will happen down the road."

"What issues?" I said, ignoring that tugging in my gut. "I am really healing, Dr. Stewart. Really."

New place, new space. I was healing. I had a purpose. I had a chance. I started playing with Garrett and Gabe. I even learned how to catch using a baseball mitt.

~~~

Age Eighteen

After a few social nights at SCAD I'd figured out who the druggies were and did my best to stay clear of them. It turned out I could go out and enjoy a few beers and go home. My new addiction was painting. I even noticed how the word, p-a-i-n, was embedded in the word painting and used that to work through so many of my feelings, as Dr. Stewart had shown me. I knew with every part of me that I would never go back to the drugs. I knew now that I would never need them again. But what *did* I need? Love? A chance for a happy life? A family of my own? I wondered some days if I would ever be able to move on.

~~~

Age Twenty-One

By my senior year at SCAD some of my pieces caught the attention of one of the top rated teachers at school, Professor Janke.

"You remember that field trip," he asked one morning after class, "over to see the Angela Jackson Art Gallery?"

"Oh, yes!" I indeed remembered.

"That is some collection your friend has there!" I pointed out in admiration.

"Well," he continued, "I'd like to take you over, to meet her personally."

He paused, reaching out to hold my arms with his hands, commanding my attention. "I think your work is worthy of being shown at her gallery. I think it is worth it right now."

I gasped, "Are you kidding me?"

Shaking his head, smiling, he spoke. "Nope, kiddo, I mean it! So let's get you an appointment."

I could not believe my ears. The Angela Jackson Art Gallery was by far the most reputable in all Atlanta, in all the Southeast really. This was insane!

"But, but," I stammered, "I'm not ready, I'm not sure."

Back at his desk, he turned.

"And I *am* sure, Jenni. Never surer." His confidence was so strong. I had to sit down to think. He flipped open his cell phone and made the call, right there, right in from of me!

~~~

Age Eighteen

There had been on other field trips at SCAD. It was the one during my first year that I remember so well.

"Don't leave anything behind that you want to use *outside* of our regular supplies in class," barked the teacher. "The regular supplies have been packed and are loaded on the bus already."

I knew we were going to Desoto Falls near my family's old homeplace in Lumpkin County.

"Take your things and start hiking," the teacher instructed when we stopped in the parking lot. "This is a you-find-it-you-paint-it type of exercise. And remember! Painting has long been revered as the fountainhead of all of the fine arts!"

A group of us laugh, as this adage is told so often by her that it is now the official mantra of our class. So this is what we chant in unison as we head up the hill.

"And be back in two hours!" we are reminded once again.

Most of the class began searching around for different views of the falls at the halfway point. Others made their spot at the platform not quite at the top. I kept going. A tree limb pulled at my hair. A climb up the sheer rock attempted to send me back down, sliding, scraping. A paintbrush rolled downhill landing at the bottom. I eyed it momentarily, but kept going up. All the way to the top.

"Don't go any farther than the top Little Nugget! Wait for us there!" I could hear Pappy calling.

When l planted my foot on the final stone, I looked out and drew in a deep breath. Again, I got what I'd earned. The waterfall flowed with force, a long woven ribbon through the rocks. The highest point was like blown glass rounding over the stone orbs. Dropping in mid-air the water changed to a curtain of silken milky-white angel hair.

"God's crayons," I said aloud. "They are everywhere." Here is where I would paint.

I hadn't been to the homeplace since I was a teenager. It was time to visit —it was time to go back. Back to my roots.

~~~

Age Twenty-One

The day of the appointment Professor Janke drove us in his car. I was about to be introduced to *the* Angela Jackson, renowned art gallery owner and curator! As we pulled into the parking lot, I panicked.

"Why don't you just take my work in; you can show it to her, and I can just stay here. She doesn't need to meet *me* really, just to see my work." I was blubbering.

"Look here, Jenni," he began. "All artists are nervous about someone like her, someone of her caliber, seeing their work for the first time. And the second time. And the third time. And the fourth time. Do you hear me?" I looked over at him, not really getting it at all.

"It is natural for you to be nervous," he said calml y. " But Angela likes to meet her artists, as much as see their work. If you get placed here, as a new-and-unknown, she expects you to spend some time in the gallery, marketing your work. She has to meet you."

I looked down at my hands as I sighed. They were newly scrubbed, clean of oil paints and manicured just for this visit. Janke opened his car door and came around, opening mine. Not another word was spoken between us as he reached in the trunk. He pulled out the portfolio with the three pieces carefully chosen for this meeting. I was remembering my father and the first time I'd ridden a bicycle without training wheels.

Well, Daddy, I thought, missing him terribly, here I go again!

Through the front warehouse window I could see the showroom. It was vast with white walls and white painted metal beams rising high up into the twenty-foot ceilings. Walking through the front door, I immediately see a smartly-dressed, thin, balding man behind a bright red desk.

"Hello," he greets us, looking up and standing at the same time. "Oh, Professor, it's always so good to see you!"

"And you, too, Slaton," he replied.

"And who do we have here!" Slaton exaggerated, with each word getting a move of its own. He stepped forward, leaned a bit to the side and outstretched both of his spindly hands.

"This is Jenni Benson, student and artist *extraordinaire*," Janke lobbed back. "We have an appointment to see Angela. I believe she is expecting us," he said, not moving at all. Slaton, on the other hand, seemed unable to stay in one spot for even a moment.

"Of course, of course! I'll tell her you're here!" he said sweetly, half pirouetting back to his desk. I looked up at Janke, my eyes questioning this Slaton guy. He gave me a knowing wink and I had to repress a small giggle. When Slaton was out of earshot, Janke whispered conspiratorially, "Just wait till you meet The Angela."

Angela was as loud as Slaton was fidgety.

"*Maaaaaarrrrk, darling!*" she intoned from her office door.

"*Come in*," she commanded, "and Slaton, get us some waters, I am *parched* in here today!" Turning, her fabulous red hair followed her back into the office with us trotting quickly behind. I had no notion of how this meeting would change my life. Forever.

It quickly became evident that Angela would do most of the talking from that point on. And little did I know how she could talk! Angela said that my scene-scapes had depth and color— definition of the Matisse style, but clearly not as intricate as a Da Vinci. Even though we all knew she was exaggerating, because that is what Angela did—it seemed that was what everyone did in here—but it worked! To have my name in the same sentence as The Masters was exciting! Inspiring! And it was her way of complimenting me.

"Who are your greatest influences young lady?" she asked me directly.

"Well, Ma'am, at one time my studies were more influenced by Rosa Bonheur the French realist. She concentrated on animals, mostly horses."

"Um hmm," she murmured. She was as quiet as I would probably ever hear her.

"I like to go way beyond," I continued with some confidence. "Like Monet, I love the landscape. But like Bonheur, I prefer to think

I paint all the way through the scene, all the way until you simply could not see any farther if you were standing there in person."

"Yes I do see that!" Angela commented in agreement. "Your scenes are alive; like you could step into them as you might step up on a curb. And this one here," she said, turning her attention to another easel. "You call it *God's Crayons*?" she asked.

"Yes, *God's Crayons*. Well, this one is inspired by my Pappy from when we went on a hike. Long ago," I summarize not wanting to say more.

"Well you could have easily called it *Fire Valley* what with the vibrant images of flames coming up through the tree line."

I couldn't speak. Fire? In God's Crayons? Had I put that there?

"Miss Benson, is that what you'd intended?" she asked, seeming pleased with her discovery.

No, it was never what I'd intended. But that's not what I told her.

"It is inspiring that you see even deeper into the scene than anyone has before," I decide lamely.

No! Where had those flames come from? They were right there! Now even I could see them. Maybe Dr. Stewart was right after all.

"Yes, Miss Benson, I like that tremendously!" she concluded.

"What did I tell you, Angela?" asked Janke. "Is she ready to show or is *she ready to show*!"

I became lost in my mixed up thoughts. Am *I* ready to show? How can I be, when I don't even see the imagery in my own work? The fire? In *God's Crayons*!? I stayed quiet—pushed those thoughts right back under that old rug, right where they belonged.

Back in the car, when I commented on her vibrant personality, Professor Janke said, "Yes, well, listen up. There's the Michaelangelo, and then there's The Angela!" We both laughed with relief that the meeting was over. But I still could not get over the flames. How had I *not* see it before? Right there in *God's Crayons*? Was there fire in those mountains? Or was the fire still in my mind, lapping up, flames not quite put out. Glowing. Waiting.

~~~

The Night

The embers—they lasted for days. The man with the kind voice was still here. Still here, asking questions. No one else was allowed around the house except the firemen in their big brown boots with coats that shimmered in the sun. Shimmered, reflecting the sun like fire, an ironic reminder. On that sunny day they seem like little dolls happily tromping though the ashes as if on a day hike. The very same men who risked their lives just days, really just hours, mere hours ago. Glowing. Waiting.

~~~

Age Twenty-Two

Ashton Holt Parker Jr. That is his name. He drops in at the gallery weekly now, to see if I have put in any new work, Angela tells me.

"Yes, Jenni dear, that young man came by again. He is a handsome one! You should really try to be here when he stops in next time," she said with a grin.

Angela was larger than life, a real Southern personality and she was gracious to me with her time.

"Jenni, darrrrling," she drawled one day, "a few of your pieces have sold and I need some media attention around here."

She was a master at getting attention indeed and, as usual when I was in her presence, I just nodded and mmm-hmmed along.

"So, I propose an event. An emergence—the crowning debut of Angela Jackson's genius discovery of her latest greatest find: the unveiling of," she spoke with a fervor, throwing her arms in a wide arc, her emerald green shirt sleeves swirling with her movements. "Of, drum roll: Jenni Benson!" she finished with a flourish. My jaw dropped and my eyes pleaded,

'No!' but she took no notice of me at all. And there she left me, aghast, as she hurried into her office to begin making the arrangements.

~~~

Age Twenty-Two, Six Months Later

The day Ashton and I met was at the great unveiling. The guest list was honed to get the finest faces of the city in the *Art Atlanta* magazine alongside her gallery's praises. It was a full-blown media circus and I was a bit confused by it all.

"Jenni Benson?" he queried.

Sometimes, overwhelmed as I was then, I forget that I had dropped my family's last name, Gold, and had taken my aunt and uncles' —Benson.

"Yes," I replied, turning to look at the deep voice behind me. Instantly the gears in my head switched. They went into slow motion watching his eyes dance while his lips moved. "It's an honor to meet you, Ms. Benson."

Angela was on target; he was indeed strikingly handsome, tall and broad with an open smile.

Snap back, I alerted myself. "Jenni. Call me Jenni."

Ashton, I would learn later, admitted that he wanted to blurt out "You are more beautiful than your art work!" But wisely instead said, "Ashton, call me Ashton. And your work—it's breathtaking. It reminds me of a piece my parents have had for a long time, it is uncanny."

Just then Angela called out in her exaggerated southern drawl, "Oh, Jenni dahling, do come here. I'd like you to meet someone."

"Yes Angela," I answered. Turning back to Ashton. "It was nice to meet you. Looks like I have to go."

He glanced at Angela and back at me, barely getting the words out, "It was nice to meet you as well," before I was being ushered across the room and out of sight.

~~~

Will Hardy

After The Night

Weeks later, our team of detectives sat Jenni Ann down at what would be her last official interrogation with us. I was in charge. Once the formalities were over the room cleared quickly. It was just her and me. Her aunt had stepped outside the room to answer the seemingly endless and pressing messages and was busy talking with a client on her cell phone. Realizing this meant she wasn't going anywhere just yet we sat there together.

"I see they appointed you a psychologist," I spoke first.

"Yea," she answered non-committedly.

"I know you've got your aunt there," I said nodding my head towards the door. "But talking to a doctor is not such a bad idea, you know."

"Mmm hmmm," she mumbled back.

"I should know," I said sadly.

She looked up and glanced sideways at me.

"Anyway," I said getting my papers together. "I'm Detective Hardy and here's a card if you need anything."

I wore my signature cheap brown suit, crumpled with wear.

"How do you know about those kind of doctors? Are you a killer too?" she asked as if suddenly seeing me for the first time.

Scraping the legs of the old wooden chair on the floor I turned to face her before answering.

"No, Jenni," I said quietly with a little snort. "I am not a killer and neither are you."

She looked back down at the floor.

"What I meant was I have no family," I continued, "Not anymore."

I looked down a bit, somewhat embarrassed about my forthrightness on this subject.

"Oh," she said without enthusiasm. "So how come?"

"My mother and father passed away long, long ago."

"Oh," she murmured, briefly raising her eyes to meet mine. "No brothers or sisters?"

she asked. I knew she must be thinking of her little sister, trying not to show her aching heart.

"Somewhat," I answered.

She looked up, more curious now. "Somewhat? You either do or you don't."

"Okay, Jenni, that's fair, so I'll tell you what 'somewhat' means. When my parents couldn't have more kids after me, they adopted. You see, they brought me home a little brother. But he just wasn't right in the head. They tried and tried, but something was clearly wrong."

I paused.

"What was he sick or retarded or something?" she asked.

I couldn't help letting out a small laugh.

"No, he was not sick, *per se*, or retarded, and by the way," I said, lowering my voice as if conspiring with her. "These days it's referred to as, 'mentally challenged'."

She let out a breath, "Yeah, I know that, sorry," she said, looking out the door where her aunt was still talking on her cell phone and now pacing.

I looked out as well, saying, "It appears that we have another minute, so I'll tell you about my brother. His name is Mark and he never really fit in. Everything was always a challenge and finally one day, when he was seventeen, he got tired of trying. He left and never came back."

"Oh, that sucks," she said earnestly.

It was strange, but with this child, this Jenni Ann, I was finding it important to help her, and to do that I had to say what was really on my mind.

"Yep," I agreed.

Just then her Aunt Lyn leaned in the door, holding the cell phone to her chest, indicating with a tilt of her head that it was time to go.

"Well, 'bye then, Detective Hardy," she said, reaching out to shake my hand.

"You call me if you ever need anything, okay?" I said, again offering my card. This time she took it.

"Wounded comrades like you and me, well, we need each other," I said sincerely. "Remember that, Jenni Ann."

As I watched her walk down the hall and turn to the elevators a memory came back to me from long ago as a young police officer. "I'm going to find Mark, if I have to become a detective myself," I'd told myself then. Back when I was lean, my haircut was sharp and my suits bore no grease stains that now were the norm from fast food joints. I'd always thought if I just learned *how* to find somebody that I *would*. But that still had not happened. After nearly twenty years I found that detective work took a lot of time and energy out of me. I was less motivated over the span of time. I thought again about the days when I'd had a family. I looked on Jenni Ann with a great sadness. I mean, she had a family one minute, and then, she didn't. Poof! Just like that. Would I worry about her like I did my brother? Will she become another casualty added to the backdrop of my life? Or maybe, I thought bitterly, if I worry about her it would mean that I didn't have to face worrying about my brother, someone I might not even recognize anymore, even if I did find him.

In another part of the building they were very busy as well. It seems the public relations department amended my final report. They thought it best to leave out some parts about the incident. To leave out the part about the house alarm not being set due to an errant teenager. They were trying to shelter her. They were idiots.

It was all over the news and all in all the papers. The headline read simply: **Family Slain: Teen Found Alive**

~~~

Jenni Ann

Age Twenty-Three

The first calls came to me through the gallery.

"Jenni," drawled Angela. "You have another message from that boy."

"What boy?" I asked, knowing I had no other messages that came through the gallery but customers and vendors.

"He says his name is Ashton, like Ashton Kutcher, and if it *is* that hot Hollywood boy, you just send him over to me!" she cackled in her raspy high-end manner. I wouldn't be surprised if she was the reason they came up with the term 'cougar'.

"Ashton!" I thought, my pulse quickening.

"Let me see those messages Angela!" I requested quickly. "How many times has he called?"

I had not been in the gallery for over two weeks since the big show. In that time he had left three messages.

"He is not interested in speaking with me, nor anyone else here. He was quite specific. I think he likes more than just your art, darling," she said with a sly wink.

I pulled my cell phone from my pocket and stepped outside. I was tingling as I pressed the numbers.

When Ashton answered it was with a blunt, "Ashton Parker."

"Um, hello, Ashton Parker" I mimicked back, all business. "This is Jenni, Jenni Benson, from the Jackson Gallery, returning your calls." This seemed too formal and I began to feel foolish for believing Angela. I was pacing and reminding myself to breathe at the same time. Did he want to talk about my artwork? Was he interested in me for something more, as Angela suggested?

"Wow, Jenni!" he softened, now sounding like the Ashton I'd met almost two weeks ago. "I am *so* glad you called me back."

"Yes," I exhaled, "Angela mentioned that you had called, a few times, actually."

"Oh, no," he lamented. "Please don't think I'm a stalker. I just wanted to be sure not to miss you, you know, in that you don't exactly have a set schedule to be in the gallery or anything."

"Well, all of my stalkers usually call a *lot* more than three times to get that kind of status," I said, easing the conversation along so that we both laughed.

"Good to know," Ashton continued. "So, tell me how the show went?"

"Well," I started, "it was great! I've never had such a whirlwind of media in my life!"

I lied. Way back then, when I'd moved to my aunt and uncle's, the media had hounded us for weeks. I pushed that thought away, back away where it belonged.

"By the time we said goodbye to the last media-mutt," I rambled, "I was exhausted. But Angela is amazing. I mean, she does this like she is having tea and scones with the Queen of England. Everything always falling in place."

"Yes, Angela is really something," Ashton said. The way he hovered over the word "something" made us both laugh.

"So," he asked, "do any of these 'stalkers' you speak of get to take you out to dinner or is that reserved for the ones like me who aren't quite up to stalker status?"

I stopped pacing altogether. I had not gone out on dates very much and, even when I did, I had no desire to further any relationship beyond the most casual. It was very hard for a damaged girl like me to find my prince out there. This one seemed different. I could feel it in my bones.

"Um, well," I stammered for a second. "Why yes, that would be nice. Yes, dinner would be nice." And our first date was set.

"Great," I thought. "I lied in the first conversation I'd ever had with Ashton." Maybe he wasn't going to be so different after all, so it seemed almost all right. Almost.

~~~

Age Sixteen

It wasn't long after *The Night* that it started. They would buzz about outside what was then my new home with my aunt and uncle. The media trucks with the reporters sitting inside—waiting. Waiting to get news in on the **Teen Found Alive** story. They would sit out there for days and nights. If it was nice enough, they would lean against the news trucks, emblazed with each of their affiliates' call letters, matching the bold letters glued to the microphones, so that anyone, everyone, watching, would know which station brought you the most up to date turn of events. So you would know which outlet could magnify any piece of minutia and turn it into something incredibly news worthy. Sometimes they would stroll and chat with each other drawing straws to see who would leave to go get coffee. Because what if something happened, something big, while one of them was gone? They were relentless in trying to get more of the story.

I was in the back seat of the car sitting directly in the middle with a sweater pulled over my face to avoid the cameras. Aunt Lyn was trying to back out of the driveway.

"Mrs. Benson! Mrs. Benson!" some called out as they all crowded as close as the law allowed.

"We hear that maybe the girl didn't set the alarm that night. Any truth to that?" shouted one of them through the glass of the car window.

"What about the fire? Did the girl set the fire?" another one yelled.

"Mrs. Benson, what about the rumors that the alarm wasn't set? Mrs. Benson!" a different one yelled over the last.

She drove on, barely looking at them through the closed window. I could tell it rattled her but she would never let them know.

"Shouldn't we just tell them?" I asked shakily after we'd cleared the gauntlet.

"There is absolutely nothing to tell," Aunt Lyn said. "And anyway, at this point it's not up to us. If the police had wanted them to know they would have told them."

And there it went, back under the rug.

But these reporters—they wanted more of the story. More details than the police would allow. More from the teen found alive.

Yes, I'd been in a media frenzy before. A long time ago.

~~~

Age Twenty-Three

"Sushi it is!" Ashton says as he politely opens the door, ushering me ahead. At my request we were entering Bishoku, the best sushi restaurant in Atlanta.

The chefs chant a greeting to us as we enter. Ashton nodded with me in acknowledgement, then leaned in to me as we are seated, asking, "Do they always say, um, Irasshaimase, or whatever it is they just said?"

"Irasshaimase?" I repeat back under my breath, laughing at his English interpretation.

Just at that moment two more couples come in and the familiar greeting is chanted aloud to them as well.

"So yes, I take it they do," he grins.

"It's like when you walk into a Walt's Ice Cream shop." I explain. "They all say, "'Welcome to Walt's!' You know, it's just a greeting."

"Oh, thank goodness," he said with exaggerated relief. "I thought they were saying, 'He looks like a cheap tipper. Give him to Shanghai Shirley in the back!'" Now he is grinning from ear to ear.

"That's ludicrous!" I laugh at the thought of anybody thinking he could look cheap in any way.

"Ludacris? The famous rapper? Where?" he says looking around jokingly.

I couldn't help but laugh at his quick wit as the waitress offered us the sushi menus.

"Well, it seems I don't know a tekka don from a unagi!" he admits, reading from the list. "Maybe you could offer some suggestions?"

"Someone as worldly as you doesn't eat sushi?" I asked.

"Eat, yes. Order, no."

I helped him navigate the menu and order for both of us. When the food arrived I identify some of the items on our plate.

"This is hamachi, or yellowtail. And this on top is ijura. It's salmon egg," I said as I showed him the plump orange translucent orbs.

"Well, in Russia, that would be known as caviar!" he said proudly. "And I *do* love caviar." He is clumsy with his chopsticks and doesn't get a bite.

"And this," I continued, "*this* is the Jackie Roll, Bishoku's signature roll."

"Ahhh speaking of, I did learn this," he said moving on with his attempts to snare the Jackie Roll. "Bishoku, translated, means 'beautiful dining.'" He is desperate to keep his slice of sushi in between the chopsticks, but instead is dicing it and renders it in a pile on the small ceramic Japanese plate.

"Well, reporter, you have done your homework, but not your handy work," I laugh again. "This delicious roll is named after the owner! You should really give it a little bit more respect," I said jokingly.

"Oh, I know, but I mean, who can eat with these things," he said, lifting his chopsticks in the air.

"Here," I lean over to him. "Let me show you how." As my arm brushes against his I can feel the strength of his physique and it makes me blush. He looks up at me. Our faces are so close. I can see his eyes change from laughing at his own clumsiness, to magnets, pulling us closer. Suddenly heat is searing through me straight to my soul with a desire I hadn't felt in such a long time. The clatter of my dropped chopsticks breaks the spell.

"Uh, oh," I stammered, leaning to pick them up off the floor.

He placed his hand on mine briefly. "No," he says as he leans to retrieve them. I notice my nails, still with bits of paint flakes adhered to them, and am struck by the contrast of his, so well-manicured.

"Maybe we should just get you the kids' chopsticks, already tied together," I said nervously while leaning slowly back into my seat.

"So, I'll use the kids' chopsticks! Tell me, when did you know you were an artist?"

"Oh," I said, relieved to be talking about something else. "Maybe when I was young..." No one has ever asked me that. I thought harder, wanting to answer. "That is an excellent question," I finally said thinking of Pappy and God's Crayons. "Maybe I don't even know."

Our conversation laced in and out of this subject and more about his job as a political correspondent. It was weightless. It was easy. The other diners were barely there. As we walked back out to our cars we noticed that the lot was nearly empty.

"Well next time," asks Ashton, holding my car door open for me, "would you allow me to pick you up, or am I still on pre-stalker status?"

Next time! I thought. He was already talking about next time!

"I'll have to Google 'pre-stalker status' to be 100 percent sure," I said, giggling as I step to the inside of the door. As I turned to thank him for dinner he reached out gently and drew me close to meet his lips. Briefly, gently. I am melting. We step back, slowly, looking into each other's eyes.

I'd long since given up on Cinderella and her never-to-be found Prince. And yet...tonight...I wondered.

"Yes," I said aloud trying to recover. "I believe you may pick me up next time, Mr. Ashton Parker."

He watched after me until I am almost out of sight before opening his car door. I know this because, using the rear view mirror, I can't help but watch him too.

~~~

Age Twenty-Three, Four Months Later

Ashton is more than just a political correspondent. He is a freelance writer and an avid art lover. He, like me, would choose to be outside given the option. On one of our walks down by the Chattahoochee River, we had a lively discussion on the current state of affairs in our country.

"I mean every commentator, no matter what side of the ticket they are on, is convinced that we are on the brink of disaster," he complained one day. "I agree with many individual points, but, hey, look back at any historical political event!"

"Well, I'm not as up on that really," I say, hoping my ignorance doesn't show.

"Oh, what *am* I ranting about? Those old blowhards will probably still be having these same debates years from now!" he exclaimed.

"Take, for example, two hundred years ago right here in Georgia," he said with excitement. "The folks in Lumpkin County were fighting with the folks in Fulton County about the gold rights in the North Georgia mountains. The Dahlonega Mint was created in 1837 because of the Georgia Gold Rush. But after only twenty-four years, it shut down, due to the Civil War."

"Oh, really?" I said, pulling my auburn hair back in a tighter pony tail. "I know a little about that area."

"After the Confederates took over in 1861, they minted gold coins for one year. Just one year," he said with more exuberance. "Now, of that gold, about 1,500 1861 D half eagles were struck. And they all went missing," he said, his hands talking right along with him.

"Missing? But 1,500 half dollars, that's $750, so what's the big deal?" I naively asked.

"Well, it was because of the rarity of those coins. The Feds were called in, but no one was talking. It created a lot of political discord. The value was ten-fold the amount they were struck for. Some estimates say it would have brought the town about six million dollars of much needed revenue after the war."

"Ohhhh," I conceded. "Six million is totally a different story!"

"Yes, it is," he said with not just his hands but now his arms becoming more and more part of the conversation too. People were beginning to notice. "It might have made them the Atlanta of the state, but instead, the area stayed rural and socio-economically unsound for another hundred years. Slowly, the town made itself a bit of a destination and some recovery is evident there now."

"Oh, Ashton, that is too ripe to be true!" I said getting caught up in his story. "Are you sure? I mean, I've lived in Georgia all my life and I don't recall any stories like that."

My family homeplace was up there, I thought to myself. Why wouldn't I have heard about this?

Ashton continued, "No, no, no, you haven't even heard the whole of it!" he bellowed now, attracting more attention. Some children looked confused and others were laughing at him. Almost as a re-enactment, with anyone within hearing distance as his rapt audience, he retold more of the mountain lore. "The story goes that there was a family up there fighting their neighbors, claiming some fault with the deed and a question of who owned what property. Record keeping was not at its best back then and some deeds got transferred but never recorded. The townspeople knew good and well that the family—I think it was the Thomases—used squatters' rights to get the land they still hold, all the while claiming that the adjacent neighbors' property was also theirs."

"Ashton, come here or you'll need a soap box," I said, laughing at his antics. We made our way over to a bench beside the riverbank.

"It seems there was some talk," he said more quietly now. "Talk of the gold being buried, somewhere up there, up on the property. "

"Wait, wait," I said, holding my hand out as if to stop the traffic of information. "I'm so confused, whose land is whose?"

"Well, that doesn't really matter. Here is my point. My point remains that the courts upheld the deed of record in favor of the other family. And then," he whispered as if he had just gotten a spicy secret story. "Fable has it that the Thomases burned down the courthouse with every single recorded deed, the remains wafting up to the sky. Sailing away in ashes."

~~~

Age Sixteen, The Night

Ashes, I feel it as it burns in my nostrils and my throat. My eyes, exploding like firecrackers with the sting.

I should have been there to save her! To get her and tell her to run! Get out! Instead, she came to the open door just as the second blast knocked Mom across the bed and then sent her sliding down to the blood stained carpet, stopping beside my father.

"Mommy? Daddy?" She stood there helplessly, with her blankie in her hand.

"Jake," hissed Henry. "I'm gonna get whatever's good to git. You take care of the girl."

Jake grabs her buy the upper arm, and goes to "take-care-of-the-girl."

He is a monster. I would give anything, absolutely anything, to change places with my sweet Abigail that night. Oh, Abigail how I wish I'd come home sooner, or never, never, ever left! I could have saved you, at least I could have saved you! I just know I could have saved you Abby-Goose! She is too young and too innocent for what fate that vile monster forces on her.

"NO!" she screams. "No don't hurt me!" Again and again.

My heart is breaking. Breaking right through my ribs, breaking right through my skin. Breaking out of my chest. I don't want to feel anymore.

As that vile monster lifts himself from Abigail, fastening his belt buckle, he turns. She is crying; he slaps her across her cherubic face. With no more thought than if he were playing with a water gun he shoots her with one bullet. Bam. *Then, just as they were leaving through the garage door, she cries out again. Was she calling out to me? Oh, God where was I?*

They grabbed the gas cans in the garage. After lighting the place, they fled. It was a while before a neighbor smelled the smoke.

~~~

Age Twenty-Three

When I wasn't in the gallery or painting, I was out with Ashton. Our love had blossomed as slowly and surely as the first kiss. From the beginning, I had introduced my aunt and uncle as my parents. It wasn't so hard, keeping up the ruse. They had taken over and without them I would be lost. It was the day of my aunt's birthday. After a celebratory brunch we crossed over to the park. Garrett and Gabe were running around the ball field, sliding on the grass in their newly pressed slacks.

"So, you really like this young man, this Ashton?" asks Aunt Lyn.

"Yes," I said, looking over at him as he chased the boys playfully. "Yes I do. Do you like him?" I ask, needing her approval.

"He has quite the resume and despite all of that political mish-mash, I really like him, too, Jenni Ann. I really do," she said sincerely.

Quietly, just to her, I admit, "I think he might be The One."

The shake of her head and the smile on her face that followed told me she thought so as well.

"Now is not the time, but, Jenni Ann, hon, you know if he is, as you say, The One, then you'll have to talk to him. You know, tell him..." she let her sentence wander just as Uncle Charles was crossing back over to us.

"I know," I agree hesitantly. I watch as Ashton tags Garrett. When he plays he is just one of them. No pretense. No lies.

I bite my lip and add, "But not now. Not yet."

~~~

Cape Cod

Ashton's family was from Yarmouth, Massachusetts on Cape Cod known by the locals as simply The Cape. I would learn that this is where the well-to-do keep their yachts and summer homes. Turning down the drive I could make out the top of the cedar-sided historic home where Ashton grew up. As we get closer, I could see the glimmer of the Cape just beyond. A blue heron is just rising from the ledge of the old dam no longer in use. Two golden Labs ran out of the side door with playful yelps leaving the screen to bounce back with a clatter to the frame. Both seem to be racing to see who will get to Ashton first, the one clearly older and the other a replica of its youth.

"Hey guys," said Ashton, bending on one knee to give them a full greeting. "Hey, my fellas."

As they jumped up to sniff me, Ashton tries to keep them off.

"Hey, guys, off! No!" But they are quite rambunctious and almost impossible to thwart.

"It's fine," I said, smiling, remembering Minnie and Racer from the homeplace. "I love dogs!"

"Ashton, is that you?" we heard from inside the screened window. We glanced at each other and the wink he offers calmed my nerves.

"C'mon, Jenni," he said quietly while holding his arm as would an escort. I hooked my arm in his and even with the dogs weaving in and out we make it to the door.

His mother is holding the door open with that big smile I so frequently see Ashton wear.

"Ashton, hello honey," she said, hugging him and planting a kiss on his cheek. She is so clearly happy to see him. I felt a tiny pull in my stomach. My mother would never again hug me and look at me with such pride in her eyes. Why have I let my guard down in this exact moment? I know I'm nervous to meet them, but I had no idea these nostalgic feelings would come rushing together, so much pain and so much love, all at once. I had to shake myself but thankfully no one noticed.

His father, a thinner and taller version of Ashton, comes striding down the stairs.

"Good to see you son!" He shakes Ashton's hand while unabashedly pulling him in for an embrace.

His mother reaches out to my hand. She clasps and then embraces it with her other hand. Not a shake really, more of a holding, as if she has a sincere desire know this woman her son is so anxious for them to meet.

"And we've heard so much about you, Jenni," she said.

"And I've heard so many wonderful things about you, too, Mrs. Holt," I answered.

"Gloria," she responded plaintively. "Please call me Gloria."

"Ash," his Father insists when we turned to each other. "Everyone calls me Ash." The two Labs are mingling in with the extended hands. They are slobbering and sharing an old, dirty, half unpeeled tennis ball—certainly a special toy brought from some super-secret hiding place in the yard.

"And this is Herbert, who clearly approves of you, and Hoover, his cohort in crime. Come on in, come in," Ash ushered.

Gloria was somehow shorter than I thought she would be and compared to my five-feet, nine inches, I feel a bit like a giraffe standing next to her. She has fragile features and pearl-gray hair, curled up on her head with a half pony half clip. Gloria, I was led to understand, was a professional consumer consultant. When I asked what that was, they all laughed. Letting me in on the joke, Gloria said, "It means I'm in charge of the purse strings around here!"

"And we would all fade away around here if it weren't for her cooking!" Ash added cheerfully. They insisted we all have a cocktail out on the terrace overlooking the water before dinner. I soon learned that Ashton Sr., loved to play golf.

"My goal," Ash insists, "is to play every Jack Nicklaus Signature Golf Course I can! Until then, I suppose I'll just have to continue working at the University to pay for my habit."

"Yes," I nodded. "Aston tells me you're quite the history professor."

"Well, Jenni," Ash started, "I do love my history. And you, being from Georgia, you will appreciate this. I did my dissertation on Southern studies, specifically the North Georgia Mountains area. I centered my paper on the Thomas/Gold debacle and how it related to the missing money from the Dahlonga Mint."

The Gold Family! North Georgia! My mind went on high alert.

He went on for a bit, then inquired of me, "Did you ever hear of it?"

"Yes, Ashton was telling me a bit about it," I replied. "But he wasn't sure of the family names."

"Well," Ashton chimed in, "it's really Dad's story, not mine, so I might have missed that point." My mind recalled that I was a Gold, Jenni Ann Gold Cagle. But Gold is a very common name.

"Son, you're a sharp correspondent, how could you miss a fact? You are slipping," he admonished jokingly.

"Jenni, Ashton tells us you're an artist?" Gloria prompted.

"Why yes," I answered. I told them a bit about SCAD and Angela, but really what I was thinking about was the name. The name Gold.

"So," Ash interjected. "Since you are quite the artist you might be interested in seeing a painting. We picked it up, down in North Georgia— funny as it seems, kind of a side-of-the-road affair with boiled peanuts and such. It was a steal and we were pretty broke back then."

"Oh, for heaven's sakes go show it to her!" exclaimed Gloria. "I'm going to check on our dinner," she says, already headed for the kitchen. Ash led us down the corridor to the library. And there it hung. The painting. It had sweeping views of what looked like a large hardwood tree with a creek beyond. And the style of the artist! It was, as I recalled Ashton saying at our first meeting, uncanny how it resembled my work.

"You can't quite make out the name but it was too good and too cheap for us to pass up. It was our first art acquisition as a married couple," he says proudly.

I bent down to look at the artist's signature. It was too dark to tell what the scrawl in the bottom right corner read.

"So you don't know who the artist was?" I asked.

"Nope," said Ash. "We never did."

"Even in good light you can't quite be sure what is says," added Ashton.

"Well," asked Ash. "What do you think?"

I began studying it more closely. It looked almost familiar. I couldn't quite place it but it looked like someplace I'd seen before. It nagged at me.

"Well?" Ash asked again.

Was this some kind of test, I thought?

"Suffice it to say it is a bit crude, with a low quality canvas...but the painting itself—it shows some soul. It describes itself so well." I lent my brief opinion hoping that I'd passed.

Thankfully at that moment Gloria called us to dinner. A roast beef *au jus* was set on the table and the topic changed immediately. Adding some aromatic garlic potatoes and blanched asparagus erased some nagging memories for the most part. But the painting tugged at me just a bit longer. And the name: Gold. Then again, I thought, Gold is a very common name.

I listened hard, trying to stay with the conversation.

"Yes, Mom," Ashton says. "My promotion puts me in Washington more than before."

I can't focus. I wonder if Aunt Lyn and Uncle Charles know anything about this story. We never talk about the family at all. We never talk about *The Night*. We never go up to the homeplace together. Ever. Truly they are fabulous and amazing! It's just that between the boys' never ending sports games and the way those two work so hard, they never really get away much. When they do go, Aunt

Lyn always wants to go to the beach. Sea Island mostly but any beach really. It's just a beach it must be. They paid for a handyman to live in the back house of the homeplace and help keep up the place. It has been in the family for so long, after all. I wondered again about the Golds of Lumpkin County. My family is the Golds of Lumpkin County. But how could I say anything. I would have to reveal my alias. Soon, but not here; not now, not while things were going so well.

They were all looking at me. What did she ask me?

"Yes, Gloria?" I say in what I hope seems an attentive voice.

"I mean don't you find it amazing how quickly Ashton has moved up the journalism ladder?" she repeated.

"Yes, yes, I do. I am so proud of him," I reply glancing over at the man who is becoming the love of my life. I swear to myself that I will pay attention. I push the thoughts out of my mind. Back under the rug. Where all thoughts like that must go.

~~~

Age Thirteen, The High Museum

"Everyone stay with your buddy and follow the docent into the museum," the teacher shouted over our heads as we piled out of the neon yellow bus.

"I wonder if they'll show any naked ones to us," giggled Lizzy.

"Oh, God, you mean like the ones with the Greek gods all lying around eating grapes with their business hanging out!" I suggested with a snicker.

"Ewwwwww, gross," Lizzy said, scrunching her nose.

We were thirteen at the time and we really *did* want to see that kind of painting.

We sounded like an off-beat symphony as we walked through the main lobby in our chunky, wedge-heeled shoes.

"First, we will start with The Landy Collection of Ceramics," our guide's voice echoed along with the footsteps as we were led to the escalators. "It is located on the second floor, so follow me."

Our bended knees parted the pleated skirts just slightly as we joined the moving stairway. The steps opened like the mouths of hungry nutcrackers at Christmastime and then closed again as we were deposited on the next level.

We entered the gallery to the left.

"The Landy Collection embodies the International Studio of the Craft Movement," instructed our guide.

"Oh, are you kidding me?" I smirked, looking around. The faces of Asian women in mosaic gave the impression of a child who has pieced together something with glue; all misshapen and slightly askew.

"Seriously," whispered Lizzy. "Abby could do better than this."

"Excuse me," questioned the guide. "Was there a question?"

"Oh, no," Lizzy said shaking her head. "We were just admiring the Asian lady." She smiled that winning smile and the herd of us moved on, following the droning on of our leader. I looked from one mosaic to the other as we strolled in our moving mass. I unwittingly began to visually morph the tiles together, blending the awkward grouted borders so that the colors came up as one piece of work. This at least made it more interesting for me. By the end of the exhibit, feet were dragging and some shirttails were clumsily becoming untucked from the boys belted tan pants as we went up another floor.

"This exhibit is called An American Century," she said, pausing at the center of the first room. As we all circled around, she continued. "This represents a variety of media on paper from the years 1850 to 1970."

"What a yawn," Lizzy whispered ultra-low, because apparently our guide knew a lot about art *and*, we guessed after being busted for the third time, had supersonic hearing too.

I put my hand over my mouth silently indicating my agreement.

Everyone was getting fidgety as the clock rounded down another half hour.

"Time for a break and lunch," announced our teacher to the relief of many.

As we ate in the commissary, it was a split between those who were glad we hadn't seen any naked art and those who still wished we could.

"It's just gross the way they ran around without clothes back then," a girl said with a condescending tone.

"Oh, yeah," a guy remarked. "What's gross is the study of the 'craft movement' and crazy drawings on paper."

"My mother says that back then, it was even more special to make art, because they didn't have the finer dyes and inks, and computers to help," said the girl with the strawberry hair.

"Hey," the boy sitting next to her said. "I thought there was a car exhibit. Wasn't there a car exhibit?"

"Yes," I replied exhausted with his stupidity. "But if you read the exhibit listings for homework like you were supposed to, you would know that it closed last week."

"Oh, bummer," he said, turning back to his ham and cheese sandwich. "Why don't we ever go anywhere with cool stuff."

As much as I thought he was an idiot, he was right. This field trip was not the bonanza I'd hoped for either.

"And now," our guide said corralling our loose huddle. "Now we will see the exhibit entitled Garden Art."

"Oh, no," I nudged Lizzy. "Yard art? At the Museum?"

"Umm," she sounded in agreement.

But Garden Art turned out to be different that yard art. It was as if the kindergarten works we'd just previously toured made way to the real artists. As if we had gone from the Leap Frog division of computing to the Mac BookPro cornucopia. One turned out to be a French Impressionist showing vibrant purple rows of lavender. Then another that trumpeted out green hollyhock in an oil on canvas. And then, turning the corner to the interior, there is was. It was the corner of the terrace in Château de Versailles. The statue, although made of stone, seemed metallic in its appearance, like shiny silver. She gracefully gazed out over the gardens, full of floral splendor. The green grass in between sits like a carpet of moss; soft and safe to step upon.

"Like springtime in Versailles," I see my mothers' smile as her voice harkened back to me. "Abby is as beautiful as springtime in Versailles." Abby-Goose. Yes, this is a beauty like that of my Abby-Goose. Pure. Graceful. Vibrant.

"This is titled *Corner of the Terrace* by James C. Beckwith," our guide said aloud, startling me. When did she get here? I looked around. Where was Lizzy?

"It's just that I notice you've been looking at this for more than a moment," she said, referring to the canvas hanging in front of us.

"Umm..., yeah," I answered somewhat embarrassed. I'd been drawing with colored pencil, but this brought so much more depth.

"Andrè Le Notre designed one of the most beautiful achievements of eighteenth century art in Château de Versailles," she continued as we both looked ahead at the painting. "The gardens took nearly forty years to complete; it is a symbol of royal absolutism."

"But this Beckwith," I queried hesitantly, for I found the landscape more than pleasing to the eye. It pulled at my soul. "He painted the gardens?"

"Oh, many, many artists, famous and not, painted the gardens. Those who were allowed access to the interior were all more famous ones, but the gardens, everyone was allowed access to the gardens."

I could now see Lizzy in the adjacent gallery alcove, staring at me dumbfounded while I engaged in conversation with our guide.

"Umm, okay, well thanks," I said looking down and then over to Lizzy.

"Thank you for your interest," she said. "We have a student rate for membership if you'd ever like to come back and see more!" Looking down at her watch, she made a tsk-ing sound. "Time to get you back to the buses!"

We moved, first like bumble bees swarming in a gelatinous unformed mass, and then, as if a thread of motion going through the eye of a needle, down the escalators towards the bus loading zone.

"What was that about?" asked Lizzy, her eyes wide.

"Oh, I dunno," I answered. "Something about the gardens in Versailles. That's in France, you know?"

"Yeah, I guess!" she said disinterestedly.

"Haven't you ever wanted to go to France?" I asked.

"Well, sure! Now that I think about it, they say the French men make the greatest kissers!" she said enthusiastically. Now that it had to do with boys and kissing, she was all in the mood to talk France. And she did, all the way back on the bus.

I was thinking about the colors in the painting and the positioning of the statue in the foreground. It was as though she was charged with a very important task; to watch over that corner of the terrace. Even knowing she was a statue, I suddenly liked her tremendously. My thoughts were quickly interrupted.

"Jenni Ann!" Lizzy was saying. "I mean, why do you think they call it 'French Kissing'?"

"And also," I added. "Why do you think they call it the 'Romance Language'?"

"Yeah," he said from the seat behind us. "And why do you think they call them 'French Fries?'"

"Whaaaatttt?" We turned and faced the back seats, our knees sitting on our seats. "You are an *idiot*!"

"But hey," he said not at all deterred. "Don't we all *looove* French fries?" Now he was laughing uproariously along with his buddies.

"*Love*! Get it! Love!" They thought they were so funny.

"Everyone sit in your seats facing forward!" our teacher ordered from the front.

"Boys," I said in disgust as we turned back around and slide back into place.

~~~

Age Twenty-Three

It was a fine New England morning. Ashton's parents declared it a sailing day. We stepped off of the dock onto the jon boat that delivered us to the sailboat moored in the harbor.

"Since you love golf so much, I'm surprised you have time for this too, Ash!" I said as we boarded the sloop.

"Ahh yes, Jenni," he smugly responded. "But this baby, this is Gloria's first love." He glances over as Gloria takes the helm.

"Yes, mateys," she says with authority. "You are all my sailors again today!" Ashton and Ash take their spot on either side of the jib.

"Jenni, you had best stay exactly where you are and *do remember*: duck down when the sail comes about!" she ordered.

"The winds are out of the north," she barks out. "Ready about?"

"*Ready!*" shout the seasoned sailors in response.

Ashton loosens the sail and with that the vessel begins moving. Looking up, worrying that the sail can't hold another ounce of wind force without ripping, I hear another command.

"Coming about!" directs our captain.

The sail is wound in and set free on the other side where Ash tightens it against wind. We sit still for a few seconds and then the sloop obeys their commands, changing directions like a wild steed. Brisk, white seaspray dances across my bare legs. Salt droplets leave themselves on my sunglasses, marking all I see as they sail, tacking across the moving waters. They are a finely honed team these three. My exhilaration cannot be contained as we zig-zag with great speed, making our way out of the harbor.

I knew it. I knew it right then. I was meant to be out, free. Not cooped up in a tiny apartment with honking traffic, car fumes and fast food wafting through my second story window in busy Atlanta. I was meant to be out at sea! Or maybe I was meant to be in the jungles! Or maybe, just maybe, I was meant to be at the old homeplace, in Lumpkin County, painting in the mountains. I looked over at Ashton. The sun shone down on his office-pale skin. He looked back at me, smiling. For that space in time things seemed just perfect.

~~~

My work, titled *Burning Gold*, was the latest in the news. It was rich with autumn leaves, golds and ambers, browns and brilliant reds, just before they lose their hold and sway gently—gracefully, rocking back and forth, as they meet the earth. In the middle of the scene is an old road, winding and never-ending. It asks the viewer to believe in it; believe in the road itself. To *know* that the road knows where it is taking you. "Come with me," it beckons.

I am very proud of this piece. Looking at the SOLD tag I realize I will be sad to see it go.

"Hello, Beautiful!" Ashton said from behind.

"Oh, hey!" I said happy to see him.

"Does The Reporter get to kiss The Artist?" he asked jauntily.

"You bet, Mr. Reporter," I answered wrapping my arms around his neck.

"It's so quiet in here," he said looking around. "Is *she* here?"

"No. *She* is not here," I smiled back at him.

"Well good then! Because I brought you a picnic!"

"But Ashton, I'm the only one here. I can't leave."

"Then it's a picnic in the gallery with my best gal!"

"I'd better be your only gal," I said laughing.

"Yep! The one-and-only! So why don't you go get us something to wash these sandwiches down with," he said as he placed the sack on the bench.

"How about water," I said loudly across the gallery.

"Sure," he answers standing and studying *Burning Gold*.

"You know, I'd like to see that in person one day!" Ashton said.

Of course, I thought. It is time to take Ashton to the homeplace.

"I don't know, you seem more the sailing type to me," I laughed nervously.

"Aye, yes," he said in his best accent. "I'd like to get me sea legs and try 'em on land, matey!"

"Is that Australian," I asked, amused with his attempt at a dialect.

"Why no," he said looking offended. "It's Jack Sparrow from *Pirates of the Caribbean*!"

I can't help but laugh out loud.

"Let's go then!" I exclaimed. "How's next week? And we'll pick you up a parrot on the way!"

"Okay then," he said looking over at me and smiling at my excitement. "Ships Ahoy!"

~~~

Age Twenty-Four

The traffic thinned as we drove up Highway 400 towards Dahlonega. Just as we left the main road, a deer ran in front of us.

"Look! A deer!" Ashton said excitedly.

"There's usually more than one," I said stopping the car.

And sure enough three more followed with a little one bringing up the rear.

"They are so quick!" he said smiling.

"Surely you've seen deer before," I said resuming the drive.

"Yeah, growing up we saw them a lot," he replied.

"It's just all the animals I've been seeing lately are the elephants and the asses in D.C," he chortled.

"Some wildlife," I commented with a grin.

We took the turn up the hill leaving the behind the shrouded road. Before we see the grove of cedar trees their scent wafts gently with the breeze through the open windows.

"This is magnificent!" exclaimed Ashton as we got out of the car. The fall colors were blazing with glory and greeted us from every direction. Ashton picked me up by the waist, twirling me around, saying, "How could you have kept a secret like this from me for so long? It is just magnificent!"

. I know, I know, I sighed thinking sadly. I surely have kept a secret from you for so long.

Ashton noticed the change in my eyes as he put me down, asking, "Hey, what happened? I didn't mean to make you sad. I love you more than anything."

"No, no," I muttered. "I love you too. It's just, well, it's just thinking about my grandparents I guess." Ashton held me tightly.

"Hey," I said, needing to break the moment. "Let me show you the pond! There are bream in there and catfish too."

"Catfish! I hope you've got some fishing gear! It'll be like on Grizzly Adams! I'll go out and hunt us up some dinner," he joked, puffing up his chest and walking with bowed legs towards the pond's edge.

"Fishermen don't hunt—they fish," I laughed.

"Ahh, well now, you see that's where they go at it all wrong," he said, shaking a single finger showing his newfound infinite wisdom.

"Okay, Jack Sparrow," I laughed as we made our way down and around the pond's edge.

He is The One, I think again. I just need a sign, a message, a hint that *now* is the time. How would Ashton take it? All the lies? That he might leave me was all too possible.

I cringed when he looked towards Old Maple.

"Hey, are those headstones up there?" he asked.

I could see from where we were that the site was covered with old vines, hopefully enough so that the names couldn't easily be read.

"Oh, those old things, yes, they've been here a while. Some precious family pets," I said. "I mean you can't even read them," I nearly panicked, thinking he might see the names, carved long ago, in the handmade headstones. If he were to begin pulling at some of the growth, I was afraid he might leave me right now. I knew this charade had to end soon. I was suddenly a bundle of nerves.

"Oh, we can get to that later! Let me show you the garden spot on the other side of this hill. Have I told you how much I love gardening?"

How would I tell him! And how would I even justify the lies? That thought alone kept me from telling all, revealing my past, right there and then.

~~~

"Okay so it's day three and I think I've got this all figured out now. I'll be down at the pond, waiting for you to come see what I've caught us for dinner," Ashton said.

"Well, you certainly look adorable in that Andy Griffith sort of way," I teased, giving him a kiss on the cheek. "But don't go expecting me to do any fish cleaning," I call after him as he heads out the door.

I began to think again about moving up here permanently. It seemed the attic would make a perfect studio when it was too cold to paint outside.

No time like the present, I think as I head up the creaky pull down stairs. First job, get a new stair system, I laughed to myself. The switch illuminates the one bulb that hangs starkly overhead. I see a few boxes stacked in the corner. As I pull the top off of the first box a blanket of dark dust slides off, landing rumpled on the floor. There are old records from the farming days: receipts of horses, milk cows and chickens bought. Of grain and fertilizer. I notice an old tin on a makeshift shelf. I reach out and take it. The crusted top is hard to remove. Are these photos? Yes! But I can barely see them. I bring them downstairs. They were not well preserved and are difficult to make out. There's one of my Pappy and Nana dressed up for some event. Another looks like a prized pig at the county fair. The next looks like a wedding photo. It is more current than the others. A wedding photo taken in the 1980s? All of a sudden it hit me: it must be Mom and Dad! I look harder. It is! I had lost nearly everything to ever remind me of them to the fire. Now I see them, so young and happy, in a way I'd never seen them before. They were always my parents to me. But they had been young once, too! They were about my age when they got married.

I look out the window and I think about marriage. I think about Ashton. Oh how I want my parents here again. Sliding down my face, they come, the wet markers of the scars in my soul. Now sobbing, I ache realizing how I miss them all. With Ashton I know which way we we're headed. It was staring me right in the face through the eyes of my parents. He had to be told. He had to know the truth if we were to take that next step. I move to the transom window and look out towards the pond. I watch as Ashton casts and reels. This is the message I am waiting for. I know we can't go back to Atlanta. Not without telling him.

~~~

Age Ten

Abby and I are playing with Barbie dolls, dressing and undressing them, making them doctors and then equestrians, then switching it to a cosmetologist or a teacher. We have a Ken doll but he pretty much stays in the same clothes all the time: a black tuxedo. We reserve him for the all-important wedding processional, which is played out time and time again. Sometimes he has shoes, sometimes he has only one, and sometimes he doesn't have any at all. But otherwise the outfit stays the same.

"Here comes the bride," we chanted. At the finale at the end of the aisle, we make sure they have The First Kiss. Then, we would break out into cheers and giggles.

"Would you ever kiss a boy?" Abby asks.

"Oh no!" I exclaim. "That is too gross!" And we laugh and make sputtering noises, disgusted by the mere thought of it.

I must have been ten, and she was four little years old.

Oh how I crave to see my family, and my sweet sweet little Abby.

~~~

Age Twenty-Four

That night, I did it.

"That photo, see it?" I said. "That picture there, look at it." I demanded of him. I was so angry. So angry that I had been dealt this deck of cards and now it was my time to show them to the one soul who I loved so much, to the one I had betrayed with my lies. Ashton sat on the couch as I stood there, shaking the photo in his face.

"Okay, Jenni, slow down!" he said. Reaching up he took the picture from me and looked.

"That...it's...it's my parents...my real parents," I spoke haltingly. My anger gave way to weakness. How did my strength leave me so suddenly? Just when I needed it?

"Okay. So, like...what?" he asked looking up. "You're adopted?"

"No, not like that," I said suddenly crippled for words.

"Well if not like that then like *what*!" he asked with a furrowed brow.

"My parents—my aunt and uncle—they are my parents..." I lost all sense of order. It meant so much to get it right – yet with every word it felt so wrong.

"So your parents were no good and your aunt and uncle raised you?" he asked getting more agitated.

"*No!* No...my sister..." again I was unable to form the words.

"Your *sister*?" he said now clearly confused and angry.

"What is going on? Is this a game?" he said as he flicked the photo on the table.

"No, Ashton. Please. Wait. Let me..." I was losing my breath. Hyperventilating.

"Jenni, this is crazy talk. Tell me what is going on?"

I fell to my knees awash in tears. I kept saying, through my sobs, "You don't even know who I am. I am so sorry, you don't even know who I am!"

"Okay then," he said abruptly. "Then tell me. Who are you?"

"I am Jennifer Ann Gold Cagle and these are my parents. They were killed, along with my baby sister, when I was 16 years old—all because of me." I started sobbing.

"What then," he asked in utter confusion rising and shaking his arms. "So you killed your family? What the hell?"

"No, no! I love them! It was awful! And they covered up my part!" I was still not speaking coherently.

"I think what I am getting here is that you killed your family and you're not who you say you are," he recited.

"I am who I am—just my name is not my real name," I was hopeless.

Sitting and waiting for his response to all of this thrust upon him all at once was like watching glass shatter in slow motion. It is all coming at us, yet we are unable to stop the damage it inflicts.

"I think you'd better come up with some more talk because you're not talking like the girl I know. What the hell are you trying to say?" he asked angrily.

I took in a deep breath. I slowed myself down. I readied myself and I began anew. The telling was like a mighty wave smashing into me. I am fighting to make my way out to sea, with that wave crashing into me, washing me, leaving me to waste away on shore. As the telling recounted the horrific series of events, he did not interrupt. He just listened. At the end he dropped his head and shoulders.

My eyes suddenly squeezed tight but couldn't stop the fresh flow of tears. These tears were of shame and fear.

"I never meant to lie to you," I pleaded. "It's just that this is the entire lie of my whole damned life. The lie became who I really am. It just never stopped."

"Jenn, come here, baby. Come here," he reached out with both arms, as I folded into him. He fought that wave with me, right here, right now, as I told all, not omitting anything.

"I'm so sorry, sweet Jenni. You know I love you. I've got you. I've got you," he soothed over and over.

"But don't you see! I've lied to you! I've lied because I know it is my fault! And the drugs!"

"No, Jenni, no. You dealt with the drugs. And it's *not* your fault," he said so sweetly. So sure. Those words, those sweet soft loving words.

"It's not your fault, Jenni," he spoke calmly. "It's just not."

"Then why did the police cover it up? Why was the alarm issue wiped out of the report?" I asked. "Why was it so important to cover up?"

"I am sure they had their reasons," he reassured. "Wow this is just so much. Look, if it haunts you so much, well, why don't you go ask them?"

"Ask who?" I am bewildered.

"The police," he answered like a true journalist. "You know, go straight to the source."

"Jenni, the lies, the truth," he said. "It is all bungled up for you. You need to solve this in your head. You have to if we are going to be together—together forever."

We were frozen in time. Those last words were out there, sailing through the air. They were pulling our gazes back together.

"Oh, Ashton that's why I am telling you *now*. Because I *know* that we are meant to be together forever, too," I said, wanting desperately for him to understand. "Don't you see? Oh God, I'm so sorry. Now that you know, if I've ruined everything, it will be just what I deserve. I never wanted to lie to you. Oh, Ashton, I'm so sorry."

We were both exhausted from the truth of it all.

"I'd like to keep loving you forever," I finished softly. My new tears were quieter. As my head hung low I could feel the droplets soaking the front of my shirt. We were both crying now. This conversation, this horrible truth, this painful defining past had finally come out.

"I love you for who you are, whoever the hell you are," he stated holding my head and staring intently into my eyes.

"Oh, God, I love you too, Ashton Holt Parker, Jr.," I said with what breath was left in me.

As unlikely as it all seemed, Ashton and I were even closer now. We knew we were bonded even more tightly than before. Nothing was going to take us apart from each other except each other. And now we knew that was not the way we were going to let it go. We were going to be together forever.

~~~

The first phone call to his parents was another weight that had to be lifted. Ashton told the bricks and mortar of the story and then passed the phone to me.

"They want to talk to you," he said, showing no signs of how they were taking the news.

With dread, I reached out and raised the phone to my ear.

"Hello," I said, breathing in deeply and exhaling loudly, tilting the phone away from my mouth hoping they couldn't detect my obvious tension. The phone call, with the revelation that I was who I was and all that had happened to me, was difficult. But Ashton would walk by and give me a squeeze of the shoulders or a reassuring nod. Slowly and surely I was able to get out the rest of the truth. It was easier than the telling with Ashton. Maybe it would get easier after all. It was healing and terrifying all at the same time.

When Ashton Sr. soaked in the information, he said, "You know that means you might be one of the Gold family of Lumpkin County. That land you call the homeplace is likely the start of the feud that is in the history books."

"Now, Ash, Jenni has more important things to think about than that at a time like this," Gloria chastened over the speaker-phone.

"Well, Gloria," I responded sweetly. "Actually, I really have wondered a lot about that. It would make sense, but I don't really know where to start. I could ask my mom, I mean my aunt, I guess."

"Jenni," stated Ash abruptly, "let me get some hard data and send it to you. It may just be better that way."

So, Jenni Gold," Ashton said when we hung up. "Jenni Gold of the Gold Family Feud that reigned for so long here in those very mountains."

"Wow that's crazy right?" I said in amazement.

"Oh, man, wouldn't that be awesome if there *was* gold buried there?" he said sounding like a mere child.

"Shush," I said, laughing at his excitement. "That is exactly how feuds get started."

~~~

They chronicled it as best they could, restoring the record of memory to the Lumpkin County courthouse. But because it was still hearsay, it could not legally be binding in any court of law. Ash emailed this much to us that day. It seems that the townspeople remembered what had happened:

The Homeplace, September 1983

Pappy and Nana Gold went on to work their property and raise Mom and Aunt Lyn until the fireballs began. They were being launched at their home with no rhyme or reason. It was always by dark of night and never a trace of who did it. The whole family was anxious. Who would be threatening them? And why? Whoever it was they clearly meant business and so did Pappy. So he kept vigil many a night in the deer stand.

"Oh, can I do it tonight," Lori begged her father again.

"No, Lorelie," he answered again. "This is man's work. I don't want you involved."

"But Daddy," she argued. "Man or not I *am* involved! If you hadn't noticed, I live here, too! And Lyn, she's so scared she's almost sleeping on top of me!"

"Her name is Lynette and when did you two stop calling each other by your own names?"

"Daddy, you are changing the subject!" she would say exasperated.

"Your mother and I gave you perfectly good names," he would answer shaking his head. "Now look here, I've got to go over to the big mill, so I'll be a while."

Giving her a kiss on the cheek he had once more firmly closed the matter.

When nightfall came and he still was not home nobody worried too much.

"You know how that auction goes at the big mill," Nana would say to the girls. "It can get pretty busy and sometimes it takes quite a while to finish up. And it's a quite a drive."

"But, Mama," Lyn would ask. "What if something happens tonight? While he's gone?"

"Nothing's going to happen, Lynette," she reassured. "Now let's all get to bed. It's a school day tomorrow so don't go waiting up for him either."

As the house lights went out Lori sat in her bed still fuming.

I'm as good a shot as anyone in the county, she thought. And that is when she knew what she was going to do. Creeping out the kitchen door she deftly made her way over to the deer stand. She had everything she needed. "Just for a couple of hours," she thought. "Just so I can show Daddy."

She rested her nodding head on the wall for what seemed like a second. She was wakened by the sounds under the deer stand. Shaking her head she wondered how long she'd been asleep. Now she could hear muffled voices but could not make out what they were saying. They walked farther away. Then she heard it! Sjiiiiiccctt, the sound of a match against the strike pad. Boosh, a flame, and then she could see them. It was the two oldest of the three Thomas boys, Frank and Henry. Frank had a fireball in a bow-and-arrow set, prepared to blast it through the far window of the house. Lori lifted her rifle and squeezed, keeping her eye on the boy.

She was hoping to hit his arm and stop him from throwing the fireball into her house. As the shot whistled through the trees those Thomas boys were just turning around and Lori's shot took an unintended path.

"Damn, Frank, you okay? Frank?" loudly whispered Henry, as Lori was scrambling down and out of the deer stand.

The fireball hit the ground and Henry saw Frank clearly now. He was still and bleeding. Henry kicks the flaming wad with a boot toe sending it sailing down the ravine.

"Stop or I'll shoot!" screamed Lori. She was taught that if you raise your gun, be prepared to shoot. Don't hesitate, just shoot. And she had followed the rules that very night.

Henry took off running and screaming, "Don't shoot! Don't shoot!"

Lori had been on a few hunts before but not like this. And as slimy and evil as the Thomases were, they were still people.

Frank!" Lori shouted, lowering her shotgun. He was perfectly still. "Frank?"

"Lorelie, Lorelie!" her daddy was yelling, racing out the back door, his shirt tails flaring behind him and his boots untied, his shotgun in hand.

"I'm here, Daddy!" she screamed back.

"Oh no, Daddy, come here, oh Lord no," she begged as she kneeled down. "I think he's hurt real bad, I mean real bad!"

"What in the hell?" he kneeled beside her. "You're supposed to be in bed!"

"I know," she shrieked. "I'm sorry!"

"Is this a Thomas kid?"

"Yes, sir, it's Frank. But I don't think he's okay at all," she said starting to waver. "Daddy I'm scared."

"I know, but we have to try to stop the bleeding. This is no time to be scared!" he spoke sharply. "Your Mama is calling the police, so there's nothing we can do but stop the bleeding and wait. You hear me, Lorelie?" he said, seeing her face pale as he tried to keep her from falling apart.

Frank lay there for only moments dying at their feet. A coyote howled from down in the valley on that long, cold, clear night.

~~~

The Thomas family exited the courthouse in a rage, shouting threats to the Judge and the whole Gold family.

It was more than a year later, when Judge Mark Stephens, presiding over Lumpkin County Federal Court, cleared Jenni's mother of all charges.

Once the Thomases were back in their place, a family meeting was held.

"Jus' cause they are named Gold, don't mean they can *have* the gold! You boys are gonna have to avenge that killin'," growled Mr. Thomas. "They can't have our land, our gold and our kin! We'll settle this the right way!"

"That's right!" agreed Jake, not really one hundred percent sure what he was agreeing to.

"I understand Daddy," spoke Henry. "Hey Jake don't you worry, I understand."

"Okay, good," answered Jake, as he went back to rocking a bit in his chair.

"You've got to look out for him Henry," quietly muttered his daddy. "You're all he's got. And he can't make it on his own. He just came out that way and he just won't make it on his own." Looking over at Jake with a resolved sadness, they both nodded their heads. Henry wanted revenge. He swore he would get that Gold Family, every one of them, even if it was the last thing in this world he did.

~~~

Age Twenty-Four

I was astonished that my parents had never spoken of this to me. Was this the change in my mother that Pappy had talked about? Knowing how *The Night* changed me forever and I thought maybe this was what had changed her. Is this why she stopped painting and moved away? Now I began to wonder. Was *The Night*, the night my family died, maybe not such an accident at all? Was it really not my fault? Were they out to get my family no matter what?

I was infuriated. What was going on here? Why hadn't Aunt Lyn and Uncle Charles told me? What about that detective? How much did he know? It was time to revisit the Fulton County police, that detective with the kind voice and the cheap brown suit, and talk about a case, about a eight-year-old case that was never solved.

~~~

Will Hardy

Eight Years After The Night

The city of Atlanta has grown in population ten-fold since that night. But I remember it well. I remember her, a girl, a teenager, lost and afraid. I remember wanting to comfort her and knowing that no amount of comfort on that night was going to help.

I greeted her at the door of my faded beige office, grimy with the dirt of time on the walls.

"Yes, Miss Cagle," I said looking at her beautiful face. "Yes, I remember you very well."

She was clearly unaccustomed to being called by her real name, her name from before. "Well actually, Detective, it is Benson now. Jennifer Ann Benson."

I blinked my eyes and without words, indicated that she should have a seat.

"I, umm, well," she looked around. It was just me and her; the door was closed. "I'd prefer it if you'd just call me Ms. Benson is all, if you don't mind."

Her stern demeanor upon entering was waning a bit.

"Ms. Benson it is then," I responded with a smile. "And you can call me Will, Will Hardy."

"Okay then, Will Hardy," she deftly averted the casualness of it all by repeating my whole name.

"How have you been anyway?" I cut off her next attempt at announcing her mission. "I have thought about you over the years, you know! And well, well, you just look great!"

"Oh, yes, well, thank you. And you look," she hesitated. I know how I'd aged over the years. But she stopped. She looked. She opened her eyes to mine and the softening showed in her face.

"You look the same actually," she half-whispered. "Almost exactly the same."

"Oh now you are just being nice to an old out of shape detective!" I smiled, thinking of my lapsed gym membership.

She smiled back, easing in to the chair.

"So I hear great things about your art career now! Very impressed," I said with candor.

"So, you know about me? About me now?" she asked.

"Yes, Jennifer Ann Benson I am aware of your public name," he continued. "But within these walls between you and me, you will forever be Miss Jenni Ann G. Cagle."

She winced a bit at hearing her name, a name very few actually know even from before.

"Did I ever tell you how hard it was to let loose of you? I mean I've talked with your aunt and uncle a bit in the first year, but I, well, I've kept up with you in the papers too I suppose," I explained.

"I don't know what to say," she answered, the wind clearly out of the sails that had brought her rolling in just moments before.

"I know you changed your name; I know you got into a mess of trouble there for a while; I know you went to SCAD and are a beautiful young lady with a bright future," I admitted.

"Why, why would you follow up on me?" she seemed astonished.

"You and I," I said solemnly. "You and I are bound together by the loss of our families. With no way to fix it—ever."

"Yes," she said. "Yes you told me that the last day I saw you, here at the police station!"

"Well I meant it," I said. "I have wondered if you would ever come back. Come back looking for more answers."

"How could you have ever thought?" she trailed off. "Because of your brother. Because you said that you and I are kindred souls."

"That's right, Jenni Ann," I confirmed. "We want to live our lives and just move on, but we can't. It's just not possible for the likes of you and me."

"So," she asked with narrowing eyes. "Did you ever find your brother?"

Nodding no, I was reminded of the frailty of our lives. To have so much power in the police force, with so many resources and to still have failed so miserably.

"I am so sorry," she said, reaching out to me across the desk and placed her hand lightly atop mine.

I lifted my hand over hers and gave it a slight squeeze.

"That's okay," I sighed. "We just don't give up that's all. Right?"

"Right," she sighed. "And that is why I'm here! I might have some new information. But first, please tell me—why was it so important to lie?" she asked.

"Lie about what?" I answered with questioning eyes.

"I didn't set the alarm," she said sitting up on the edge of her seat now. "Why did that become such a secret?"

"Oh, Jenni, you were underage, a teenager. There are so many rules about how to handle a minor."

"But instead I've spent my whole life in a lie, knowing that it is all my fault," she was incredulous. "How can that be a good way to handle a minor?"

"That case, Jenni," I said, "that crime scene was so horrific. So brutal...." I don't want to say it out loud.

"So brutal *what*?" she asked.

"Well, Jenni, it makes my stomach turn. But there is just *no* way that that crime was random. There is no way the small oversight of your not setting the alarm, in this particular case, would have yielded a different outcome."

"Then again, *why*? You know the press hounded us and blamed me in the news stories."

"They didn't actually blame you, Jenni," I explained.

"*Yes*," she interrupted. "Yes they did! And my aunt swept it away. And, and it has tormented me for *years*!"

"Jenni, the signs are all there. It was not random. It seemed more like revenge."

"Well then *why* didn't anyone tell me?" she asked astonished.

"Your family, your aunt and uncle. They really didn't want more, well, trouble for you."

"Trouble for me," she shook her head.

"It has been nothing *but* trouble for me," she said.

"What do you want me to do, Jenni," I asked quietly. "I will help you. What do you want me to do?"

"Look at this," she said placing the documents on my desk. "It is a little far-fetched but it is a real possibility. I mean, look at the Hatfields and McCoys?"

I took the history compiled in an orderly and chronological timeline by Ashton Sr.

"You read that. You read it and you call me. I have spent so many years and lived such a lie of a life. Your departmental rules have no place anymore. I'm an adult now. Tell the truth. Call a press conference. Do whatever." And with that, she strode out.

I knew she had changed her name and I wanted her to have a normal life. I knew it was best to not contact her. But I would think of that night many times. I would think about it driving in my old Ford Taurus, the driver's seat worn with time, frayed slightly from the entering and exiting of me, its keeper. I would think about it on my shabby couch, with the empty Chinese cartons lying about and soda bottles half drunk on the dusty coffee table, the television playing some rerun of a survival reality show.

I called her the moment I'd finished reading through the report.

"Don't worry, Jenni," I assured her. "If there is anyone who is on your side on this case it is me. I'll look under every rock in North Georgia if I have to."

A relief—a chance at finding the killer or killers. This is what I wanted to give her. She needed it, deserved it! I am now her last bastion of hope. I was there at the scene all those years ago. I know.

I will not let her down, I thought. Not the way I'd let myself down, never finding my little brother. Somehow, I felt important again. I felt I had purpose. It was like a fire rekindled in my spirit. Where had those Thomas brothers been all these years anyway? And where are they now? It was time to find out.

Now I knew for sure that I was the person who could help. I again had hope, too. We were now linked together, bonded and resolved.

I made a call to the Lumpkin County sheriff who agreed to see me. Yes, tomorrow would be fine. I am due for a drive to the mountains any damn way, I thought. This city scene was getting to me.

~~~

I pulled up to the one story building. I noted the addition of some white columns in the front giving it a bit of an upgrade from it's original. Entering the station I noticed how clean the office appeared. As I looked over the gold-framed portraits of the Lumpkin County law enforcement leaders hanging on the walls I couldn't help but notice the stark difference from my office.

I smelled lemon cleaner and saw real flowers in a vase on the receptionist's wooden desk.

"May I help you?" she asked.

"Yes ma'am, Detective Will Hardy, here to see Sheriff Jones," I stated with polished politeness. As she looked on her computer screen for confirmation, I added, "I have an appointment."

The nameplate on her desk read Gertrude White. He guessed by the peeling coating of gold plastic that it was likely made some twenty years ago.

"I'll let him know. Please have a seat," she directed as she got up to go get the sheriff. I had done some homework on this guy. He'd started with the police department some twenty-five years ago, so I figured that this Gertrude White may well have been with him a long time. This meant she was either very loyal to him, or very vengeful. Like a long lived marriage, I thought glumly. I'd also gotten wind that this guy ran the whole county, despite the separate municipalities in recent times. I knew about big headed guys like this one. Everything was not always by the book with his kind.

After ten minutes of waiting I was ushered back. It seems, I thought, that I had advanced past Gertrude the Guard. Once in Jones' office I dropped a copy of the history on his desk.

"I do appreciate that, Detective Hardy, but I surely know all about that mess, what with the Thomases being such a blight on the county reputation itself. They kinda make us all look like a bunch of rednecks," he finished in his natural Southern tone.

"So where *are* those two Thomas boys anyway?" I asked. "They still around here?"

The sheriff's chair creaked as the heft of him moved it, rocking slowly back and forth. "Well, they are said to have moved on to

Habersham County some eight years ago. I know I haven't seen them around here. Shoot we don't even much talk about that crazy family anymore. They all just cracked up I tell ya'. The papa got to walking out in the woods at night, searching for his boy, and they say a mountain lion got him. And, well, let's see now. The momma, she is said to have gone stark raving mad in the old shanty until she simply just passed away in her rocker, ranting one minute and dead the next. So, then, it seems those two boys, well, they just moved on, looking for work in the Habersham area."

"Umm hmm," I nodded non-committal in my tone. "Well then, how about that tour you promised? Maybe see the Gold homeplace?"

"Sure," said the sheriff. "Come on. We'll take my truck. It'll get over the back roads a lot better that that old Ford you've got out there," he laughed looking out of the window where he had obviously been watching as I arrived.

"Yeah," I agreed while slapping Jones on the back in camaraderie. "That's the truth!" We both laughed a little too loudly, both of us not quite sure of the other, as we headed out the door.

The town was very quaint, its population numbered some 5,500 people. The square, which was the hub of Dahlonega's government activities, was well kept. There were freshly painted buildings and newly hung awnings in places that had been there for two hundred years or more.

Jones entertained me with small talk, probably scripted in his head for quite some time, about the town. I wanted more on the Thomases, but knew that this was part of the dog-and-pony show, like a required course in high school.

"You seem to know a lot about this town," I commented.

"You know, I take real pride in this area. In this place, these people and all that happens here. It's my town," said Jones with a sideways glance.

"So, Sheriff," I said, changing the subject, "what ever happened to the Thomas house?"

"Well," allowed Sheriff Jones, "it's just barely standing. It wasn't a sparkler to begin with you understand. But hey, I'll be glad to take you over there. It'll be our first stop, then, so buckle up. These back roads are rough I tell you."

It took thirty minutes to get to our destination, making small talk the whole way. The truck slowed. I looked around thinking maybe there was a deer or something. Then Jones stopped all together.

Hell, I thought to myself. I hope the sheriff is wrong and this isn't really like the movie *Deliverance* or something, where I end up dead in the brush somewhere.

"Here it is," said Jones, extending his hand so that my attention went to the hill on the right.

"What? Where?" I grunted.

"Right over there," continued Jones. "Through that kudzu patch, you can *all*-most make out the top of what was the fireplace chimney."

We got out of the truck and stepped as far off the rutted and rocky road as we could, peering over the mountain of growth.

"Here are my binoculars, Hardy," offered Jones. "It'll help a little." With the binoculars I could see the top of the chimney. Using that as a guide he figured where what was left of a house must have been standing. It was so damn dense, it led him to wondering if someone *could* just be in there.

"Sheriff, if you don't mind my asking," I asked, not really caring if Jones minded or not, "who has the deed to this property now? I mean with the parents gone and the boys having disappeared, what happens?"

"Hmm," pondered Jones. "I believe we may have to double check with the clerk of the court, but what with the Fire of 1943 burning up the courthouse, anything we have from before that is written down is hearsay. If anyone wanted to buy this land, it would go before a judge and then he would issue a notice. Trying to find whoever they *think* is the last known deed holder. If no one shows up after ninety days of real dogged tryin', then there is a process that begins. I think it takes about a year, uncontested, to claim it as yours. The county gets some money too you know, for handling this mess around here. It's only right. But we ought to make those Thomases pay for it all."

"What?" I turned my head back around. "I though you said they were destitute, backwards and nowhere to be found? How would you make them to pay?"

"Oh, of course there would be no real way, of course," Jones muttered.

We climbed back into the truck and backed out so perilously, that I thought momentarily about my Last Will & Testament. Who in this world would I leave it to anyway, what little I have? I then thought again about Jenni. What I *do* have, he resolved, is time. Time to solve this case. For Jenni.

They drove a few miles in one direction and then zig-zagged back again. The roads' surface changed dramatically making the ride instantly more tolerable.

"This is the beginning of the Gold homeplace," Jones said. "They have always kept up this property. They always have a guy to come and check up on things. And then there is the houseman who lives on the property; he fix's things up real regular like. Yep, they do pretty good."

I was nodding in agreement as we turned again, winding up the road towards a bank of cedar trees on the right. I could feel immediately how one could be at home here. It was just something in the air, or maybe the way the sunlight sliced through the old oaks and green cedars. Then the cabin came into view. It was an old split log version but not quite the country style you'd expect. It had more height. The wood rails on the wide porch were well sanded, made to fit each other so perfectly. You knew whoever built that knew what they were doing. The centuries old oak used to make the door was thick with a hammered metal front handle and knocker. It was taller than expected, with an arch spanning the top.

You must remember, he recalled Jenni telling him. Pappy was a big man.

They got out and the sheriff went to the side of the house. He reached in to a hidden cubby and pulled out a key.

"Well I'll be," he said. "I would have thought that little Miss Gold, after all she's been through, would have taken this away by now. It's your lucky day, 'cause I guess I can show you inside, too."

"Don't you think we should notify the guy you say lives on property?" I asked, not wanting to get shot for breaking and entering.

"Naw," sneered Jones. "I'm the sheriff around here and everyone knows it too," he said, his ego showing.

· When we entered the cabin what I noticed first was the array of floor-to-ceiling windows flanking the immense fireplace. The sandstone hearth held a few pictures and a dried-up flower arrangement long left behind. On the opposite wall there were built-in bookcases. The floor was adorned with a worn antique Persian rug.

Jones flipped on some lights. It was indeed a place where you could feel at home. They walked to where an addition had allowed for a larger living area and an updated kitchen. The stained glass transom over the windows at the sink looked out towards the pond and leant some peace and tranquility instantly. A sitting room then led to a hallway, allowing for three bedrooms and a bath for each.

As I looked up at the pull cord indicating an attic above, I recalled Jenni's saying how perfect it would be to put a studio up in the old attic. I reached up and grabbed the cord. With an audible creaking the wood gave way sending dust particles swimming in the air. Climbing up the old ladder steps I again thought, having had forgone my workout routine long ago, that this might be my demise. Once up the stairs, I could see that it had plenty of head-room.

Yep, I thought. Jenni is on to something. You could really see the possibilities here.

"You seen enough, Hardy?" asked Jones from below.

"Umm yeah. I was just coming down."

Now outside, I asked Jones if he could take me to the spot where Lorilei Gold had killed Frank Thomas.

"Sure, no worries there," replied Jones. We found the spot pretty easily, as the deer stand was still there, worn and graying. I looked across a mighty ravine and onward to see a kudzu woven landscape.

"Hey Jones," I shouted from up high in the deer stand. "Let me see those binoculars again!" I would swear I saw movement.

What did I just see? What was that? I thought to myself. But it was fleeting—then nothing more.

"I've left them back in the truck, Hardy, sorry 'bout that," he answered from the ground.

"Oh well," I said deflated. "Maybe this mountain air is getting to me."

"Okay then, Hardy," said Jones a bit on edge. "Time to head back then. I've got a pile of paperwork to fill out today so if you don't mind the tour stops here. As it is I'll already be glued to my desk the rest of the day."

~~~

Once back at the station we shook hands and Jones promised to keep in touch with any new information. He offered to help contact the Habersham authorities for Hardy too.

"For my report, I'll need the name of the contact up there, you know," I said with a pause. "Procedure." I no more trusted this sheriff than I could throw his fat ass.

"Aww that would be Blanchard, Mac Blanchard. No one better, straight as an arrow lawman and the folks really like him too," said Jones, clearly ready for this visit to be over. "But let me warn you: he gets a little mixed up these days," Jones snickered. "You never know if what you get is what it really is, ya hear?" He then watched as I pulled my car out of the station parking lot.

This just won't do, Jones thought. Can't have no lawman from Atlanta screwing things up for me. Not after all this time.

Jones got back in his truck and took a drive to the outskirts of town. Driving up to the backside of Brushy Mountain to the trail that led to the other side of the ramshackle house covered in kudzu, he sounded his horn two quick alerts. Henry and Jake made their way down the twisted path knowing Sheriff Jones was on the property.

"Boys," Jones started. "You are gonna have to move quick to get rid of the rest of that mess and find that gold. I'm not gonna cover for ya' and die like your daddy did, without my paradise retirement."

Henry, the oldest, understood. Jake muttered, "But how are we gonna do that from here?" Sheriff stared hard at Jake.

"I happen to know that since that girl and her boyfriend come up here more and more, the handyman has to get supplies up there for them. I'll know when he complains about it to me, like he always does, and then you two get over there and finish the job. Then start diggin'," he snarled.

~~~

Jenni Ann

The Night

*T*he neighbors wake up to the smell of smoke. They race to get everyone out of the house. Working from adrenaline they are not even sure where the smoke is coming from. Once outside they see the Gold's house up in flames. They gasp, step back and grip their children. They are all barefoot and in pajamas standing on the lawn. They back even farther away. The neighbor reaches for his cell phone in the pocket of his robe. He dials 911. A blast. Windows explode out from the second floor. The flames flicker hungrily upwards. They have to get farther away. Now there are more neighbors out on their lawns. With a deafening roar the fire trucks arrive. Big trucks with erect ladders that loom over electric poles. Firemen are shouting. Water explodes out of the flesh colored hoses. Smoke plumes pour upward—dark and ominous. The *police arrive. The questions begin. "How many live in the house?" Have you seen any of them tonight? Have you noticed anything at all out of the ordinary?" No. It is just another regular Saturday in suburbia.*

How could they ever know that just moments before, two men were passing one house over, headed in the opposite direction, on foot.

~~~

Age Twenty-Four

I reached over to grab the ringing phone. I knew it was Hardy because of the ring tone from *The Lawmen*.

"Hello!" I answered, always glad to get his updates.

"Hello, Jenni dear," Hardy said and I could almost see his smile through the phone. "Well I just got the grand tour of your mountain home."

"Oh, really," I said with curiosity. "Maybe one day I'll give you the inside tour as well!"

"Oh, no need," he continued. "That egotistical big-headed sheriff has no problem getting in."

"Really," I said in confusion.

"Yep! You really ought to take that key out of the cubby."

"Are you kidding? There's still a key in that cubby?"

"Yes, ma'am," he said. "And that ole fat boy doesn't have *any* problem using it either."

"Isn't that something like breaking and entering?" I asked.

"Oh yes indeed it is!" he said. "I ...definitely...if I..."

"What? You're breaking up! Will?" I asked to the crackling of deaf airwaves.

"Damn," I said hanging up. The reception up there was spotty for sure. I'd just have to wait for more.

As I got back to my studies of North Georgia painters from the early 1960s, I started humming the song.

The Lawman came with the sun.
There was a job to be done.
And so they sent for the badge and the gun
Of the Lawman.

~~~

The Night

Henry and Jake reached their truck on the outskirts of the neighborhood and sped off absolutely undetected. They took I-85 north and then exited on State Route 9E the rest of the way to Dahlonega. They didn't use that newfangled Georgia 400. No, it was all nice and flat and cushy waiting for the city folks. Not meant for the real mountaineers. It had no swoop and turn in the road to remind you that you were in mountain country. Georgia mountain country. It wasn't until they closed in on their normal approach from the backside of Brushy Mountain that they spoke.

"Damn Jake," started Henry. "Why'd ya' have to go doin' all that to that girl? I've told you about that before. We got gold to think about!"

"Aw to hell with you, you're always tellin' me what to do, I know as much as you!" Jake shouted back. Henry had always been the one looking after Jake since Frank was murdered by that girl and Mama and Daddy were gone.

"Jake, you're kinda slow, remember? Mama and Daddy said for me to look out for you, and that's a-what I'm gonna do," Henry said, a bit more softly.

"Yeah," Jake sullenly admitted. "Yeah I know."

They would wait a few weeks and figure out how to turn the jewelry into cash. They had ways after all this time. Sneaking and slithering was their specialty. Like when their daddy helped that slick one from Nevada. The Dahlonega Mint? Of course, their daddy had said. Everyone knew that gold had been stolen and probably spent long ago. But no, the Slicker, had said. Not at all. Look at the records. It probably sits right about here he had said, indicating with a pointed finger on the map.

What about a story of it being buried right almost here? Near here? From some thieves a long, long time ago? Well, have a seat stranger, their daddy had said. That Nevada slicker never made it back from his trip. The boys saw to that all right. And now, Henry and Jake were still waiting. They were holding that map and waiting for that damned Gold family to quit coming up here. To quit keeping up the place so they could start digging. It might take weeks, or even months. People had to quit *coming up there so they could get that gold. That gold might be buried, according to the Slicker, under what is now the addition on the Gold house. That must be where it was, their daddy had figured long ago. It is what they were told and they were waiting for their chance to get it out of the ground and live the life. They even used the Gold homeplace sometimes in the winter when it just got too cold even for them. Everyone in the county knew where the key was right? And then they could sleep right on top of what would soon be theirs. They were so close now.*

~~~

Age Twenty-Four

It keeps coming back to me—the painting in Cape Cod. I have been trying to find any history of the mysterious painter but come up with nothing. I wanted to look a lot more closely at that painting that had been purchased years ago, on a study trip for Ash's dissertation while in the north Georgia mountains. The one that was unusually like my style of painting.

"Well, I've got to be in Boston to cover the mayor's bid for the presidency," said Ashton. "You know it's only a two-hour drive to the Cape."

"Oh," I wondered. "I thought you had to be in D.C.?"

"Well, then I'll have to fly down to D.C., when Congress resumes the budget talks the next week," Ashton offered. "Why don't you fly up and meet me on Friday? We'll rent a car and head over to the Cape for the weekend. You can fly home from Boston and I can get back to the old cronies. It will surely be an interesting battle with the Democrats and the Republicans."

"Umm," I responded offhandedly, as I took little interest in politics. "So what's the battle about now?"

"It's the same old business," he stated. "And no one really ever changes much of anything but they seem to like making a show of this sequestering."

"Umm yea, that's what's all over the news," I said distractedly. "Right?"

"Riiiiight," he said looking over at me, knowing how little I pay attention to the news. "But hey, but the point is, we can go see the painting," he assured me. "Together."

"Of course, together!" I said, breathing a sigh of relief. "Thank you, Ashton," I said, pulling him to me. Looking up at his face I realize again how lucky I am to have found my true love.

"I love you, baby," I said. This painting was like a strange driving force. It had a power over me and it pulled me, propelled me with a need to see it again. I used that power, kissing Ashton, in between the "*I love yous*" that were spilling out of me, with a passion. I didn't want to go up alone. I didn't want to go without Ashton.

~~~

Boston

There was a cold biting wind when Ashton picked me up at the airport. We got farther from Boston headed south on Highway 3 as the morning sun shone in brilliantly from the east, warming me.

"What is it about that painting Ashton?" I asked, looking out as the signs for Plymouth whisked past. I immediately imagined smelling the Atlantic Ocean from where I sat, so close yet out of sight. The Atlantic was a different animal up here, up north, from the southern one. In the south, the Atlantic seems flatter, calmer. Up here, and especially on the Cape, it has a roaring fierceness, like a caged lion, wanting out.

"What is it about that painting?" I murmured again as I turn my face and lay my forehead on the window. Ashton reached over and squeezed my hand, knowing there was no good answer.

~~~

Cape Cod

Gloria and Ash had pulled the painting down and placed it in the living room where the lighting was better. Peering, with a magnifying glass, I did my best to decipher the name scrawled on the bottom. You could not make it out. Someone had scratched it out.

But you could not overlook the telling similarities to my style. The dip of the brush left behind a wide sweep of oils in rogue reds and glassy blues. The white catching the last of the trail of paint as the brush surely rose guided by the creator's hand.

"When did you say you got this?" I pushed. "Where in North Georgia?"

"Oh," thought Gloria intently. "At a roadside apple stand, as I recall. Right, Ashton? What year was that do you think?"

"We were married, Ashton was not born yet and I was working on my dissertation," he pondered aloud. "So let me think, what were the years we frequented Georgia?"

"I just cannot get over the style of this artist. It is so similar to mine. And from North Georgia. I don't know," I said shaking my head in dismay. "I just don't know what it is about this painting."

~~~

Age Twenty-Four

We had been dating for one year. To mark the occasion Ashton was taking me out to a surprise dinner and he wouldn't tell me where we were going.

"Should I dress up, or jeans, or what?" I asked.

"Whatever you want," he answered with a super-sized smile on his face.

"Well, I have to have a clue, so I know what to wear," I insisted.

"You are so beautiful, your clothes will hardly be noticed," he said, so close now that I could feel the heat of his breath on my lips.

"Sooo," I said after a deliciously long kiss, "are you suggesting I should go naked?"

"Even better!" he laughed. "Okay, so dressy casual, how's that, can you work with that?" he said to me finally as I walked back to the closet.

"Yes, I do believe so," I said, scanning my choices. "But not knowing where I'm going is tricky."

I finally chose the espresso-brown sweater dress with a wide gold belt and boots. It was cold for Atlanta, dipping into the teens that evening.

"Surely this won't be an outdoor thing, Ashton?" I called out, asking.

"No baby," he said as he came back in the room. He had been pacing nervously.

"You sure are funny tonight. Is everything okay?" I asked.

"Great," he responded. "Couldn't be better!"

As we drove towards the anniversary destination, I started playing the guessing game.

"The Ritz?" I asked.

"No, too stuffy," he answered.

"The Shack? For oysters?"

"No, too messy for a night like this," he grinned.

As we got closer, my guesses got wilder.

"To the moon?" I laughed.

"To the sun for you, Jenni—straight to the sun!" he laughed back.

Then suddenly I could see where we were going. We were turning into the shopping center, the very one where we had our first date.

"Oh my God, you're taking me to Bishoku!" I exclaimed drawing my hand to my open mouth. "I cannot believe I didn't think of Bishoku."

He parked the car so that we could see the diners inside the front window and smiled broadly.

"Ma'am," he ushered.

The chanted greeting was quite robust this time.

"Well, the sushi chefs are in quite a good mood tonight," I whispered to Ashton.

"Hello, hello," welcomed Jackie, who flowed gracefully over to personally escort us to our table. "Ashton has something special for you," she intoned, as we made our way over to the back corner, where a private, curtained room awaited us. He'd had them set it up with what seemed like a hundred tea candles so that it glowed like a million fireflies on a hot Georgia night.

"Is this okay," he asked.

"It's more than okay—it's brilliant," I said truly amazed.

We slipped off our shoes and slid into the wonderland.

"I've even been practicing with my chopsticks," beamed Ashton.

I leaned over and gave him a big kiss. Unbeknownst to us, silhouetted against the curtains, our shadows could be seen by all of the other patrons during the entire meal.

As the dessert came I leaned back on the cushions. I was relaxed and gloriously happy.

"You know," I pondered . "I think we should fix up the attic at the homeplace. You know, for my studio."

"Well of course we should," he agreed just as dessert arrived.

As I lifted my spoon to taste the green tea ice cream, I noticed a chocolate pirouette placed in each of our bowls.

"Oh, that's a new touch," I said while I lifted mine to dip in the ice cream. And there it was, placed on the stick, tied with a tiny ribbon, and gleaming like a glacier in Antarctica. A beautiful diamond ring.

My mouth stayed open. My eyes went directly to Ashton.

"Jenni, we have been through so much, and I know it's soon, but I love you. I knew you were the one on our first date, here, a year ago," he said all in one breath.

"Ashton, I...I," I stammered.

"Here," he said, taking the pirouette, and untying the ribbon. "Jenni Ann G. Cagle Benson, I want to be with you for the rest of my life. Will you marry me?"

As he slid the ring on my left wedding finger, tears began rolling down my face.

"Yes, yes, yes!" was all I could get out. It was so perfect!

It was only seconds before I heard the loud POP of a champagne cork. Jackie drew back the curtains and a rousing applause erupted from the other diners. Champagne was poured for everyone that night.

~~~

Age Twenty-Five

It was decided that we would have the wedding at the homeplace in May. Spring would be just perching up on its elbows there in the mountains and there is no prettier time, other than fall.

"Yes, Aunt Lyn, I know that we are pushing it," I explained on the phone, old and bound to the wall with a curly black leash.

"No, we can get the renovations done, it's not really *that* big. Uncle Charles drew it up, he can tell you," I assured her.

"Yes, I know you have to go, okay, okay," I answered her requests to not overload myself. "And tell the boys I love them, too!" I said, not knowing if she had already disconnected on her end before she got the message. I looked down at the phone in amusement. She was always so busy and there she was advising me not to overload.

The demolition was set to start tomorrow, just as Aston's parents were coming up to stay and see The Wedding Space, as Gloria put it.

Using the old rotary dial, I turned my finger with each number, thinking I would try one more time to talk them out of coming tomorrow.

"Gloria? Hello, it's Jenni," I began.

"Oh yes, Jenni, hello! We are so excited to see your old place, or whatever you call it, and get an idea of The Wedding Space!" she started right away.

"Well, yes, about that," I paused. "You see the contractor, he had a cancellation and the schedule changed, and it seems he really wants to start work right away, and well, that means tomorrow! I would just hate for you to see the place a mess."

"We don't give a darn about a little construction, Jenni," she persisted. "It is an adventure for us!"

"It just seems you'd be more comfortable when they are finished," I pleaded.

"Well, we have our plane tickets and Ash is pretty set to play a golf course up there, so I think we will just have to deal with it," she said, in her matter-of-fact manner that was so Gloria.

"You know, we could all get a room in town," I started thinking aloud.

"Oh nonsense," Gloria said, and I could almost see her shaking her head over the phone wires. "That's ridiculous. We are fine, don't you worry about us. And how is

Ashton?" she asked, changing and closing the subject all at the same time.

~~~

The Homeplace, Spring 1998

It was a visit in the spring to the homeplace. Our parents and Nana went to town to get groceries. My sister and I were chasing butterflies in the meadow across from the other side of the pond. We were giddy with excitement, always knowing that here with Pappy and Nana we have no worries. The field grasses had begun to show some height. Not like in mid-summer when we could run and play and our parents could hardly see us, but high enough for us. It was our jungle. A magical fortress where we are the princesses. It is a kingdom in our minds. We ran from the hob-goblins. We chased bumblebees and butterflies while the crickets jump high and fast, trying to escape the footprints of our journeys. It was that one time, when we came upon it. A small deer, a fawn. She was young, like us. She was lying on the ground, hurt. We could see the fear in her eyes as we bounded up, unaware of her presence until we were just upon her. She cried out, trying to get up, to escape. She was wounded. We could see the blood.

"Pappy, Pappy!" We screamed out while running, almost tripping over each other, to get to our anchor, our Pappy. It seems to take forever, our little legs in constant movement, our breaths audible to ourselves, so loud, even as our screams persisted.

"Whoa, little missies, what has you two in such a tizzy?" He scooped us both up, now at the other side of the pond, closer to Old Maple.

"A deer, a baby," I blurted out. "She's hurt. She's bleeding. We have to help her Pappy." Both Abby and I were sobbing, relieved to be in such strong competent hands and also scared at our finding.

"A little fawn you say? Hurt? This time of year?" he pondered. "But it's spring. Why would a deer be hurt now?" Hunting season is in the fall. The babies are just coming up and every hunter knew you let them repopulate, raise their babies. He went inside—we followed his every step—and reached for one of the rifles in the gun case. Checking to see that it is loaded, we all trooped back out at a much slower pace towards where we remembered the deer to be.

"There she is!" Abby called out spying her first. Pappy got closer and determined she'd been shot in the back leg.

"What kind of damn heartless fool would ever shoot a baby doe in spring?" he ranted angrily. Turning to look over the hillside his jaw squared tightly. "Damn Thomas boys, that's who," he seethed.

"Girls, head back to the house," he commanded. "No," we cried. We wanted to be with him.

"I'm gonna have to put her out of her misery. Now do as I say and get back to the house," he commanded again, calmly, with compassion. We did as we were told, not entirely sure what was about to take place. He stayed there beside her until we get all the way to the house on the other side of the pond, back up the hill. Then we heard it. The rifle. The single shot. He lets the young calf go as humanely as he knew how. Back in the house, we hug and cry some more. Now we knew.

"I'll never let anyone take my little fawn, my little Abby." I thought in that moment. "Never."

~~~

Age Twenty-Five

"How do you put someone out of their misery?" I cried to Dr. Stewart. "I mean Pappy did it with such compassion. How can I help my Mother? My Father?" I broke down holding my head between my hands. "My Abby? How do I put myself out of this misery?"

"Well," she explained. "One way that people do that is with a service or a funeral. It is for the survivors really. It helps us to put to rest those we love. It is a way of saying goodbye with meaning and dignity."

I looked up, red-eyed and puffy.

"It is," she continued. "It, it...gives us a place to accept our sorrow."

A month later, the truck eased up the driveway at the homeplace.

"Hello," called out the driver.

"Yes, hello," I answered leaving the large wooden front door ajar as I hurried out to meet him.

"We have a delivery for a Jenni Gold Cagle. That's you?" he asked.

"Yes," I answered with pride at hearing my name spoken aloud. "That's me!"

"Well," he proceeded," where would you like it?"

"Over there," I said pointing. "Just follow the drive."

I jumped in the old golf cart and went over the grass up the crest of the hill as they took the driveway. I passed the cedars to the back of the house nearer the creek until I arrived at the foot of Old Maple. The truck was making its way on the drive that led them down by the pond and back up towards me. The newly cleared space was next to Pappy and Nana.

"You see, it should face down the knoll towards the pond."

They both looked at me and then at the clearing on the ground.

"Like these two here," I said pointing.

"Yes, ma'am." They were quiet. Solemn.

They measured across before leveling and then setting the foundation stone. "We're gonna need to anchor this in, so cover your ears," warned the young man. The pounding of the steel bar rang out like the strong man at the circus who hits the bell every time. When the violent clanging came to an end, they deftly poured concrete and hefted the memorial stone into place. I smiled as they got out the dowels and began to screw it all together. It reminded me of a large art installation we had done at SCAD. As students, our assignment was to set up the scaffolding and secure the posts in order to hang all of the art. It was to last a week in the open-air courtyard. The second night there had been fierce thunderstorms so on the third morning we were anxious to see how it held up. Viewing the flattened package one of my classmates summed it up best. "Thunderstorm: One, Scaffolding: Zero." That's when we learned what dowels, pins and shafts were for.

"Yes," I said satisfied. "Just like that."

"Now we recommend you not sit on it or put any weight on it for 24 hours. The dowels we use will hold it but its best to let the concrete set."

"Oh," I acknowledged. "Of course."

"If you'll please sign right here," he said when they were done.

"We are so sorry for your loss, ma'am," said the driver of the truck.

"Oh, yes. Thank you," I said signing the paperwork. My Loss. Maybe someone had spoken those words to me, years ago. But only now do I hear them and feel their weight. My Loss.

I waited until I could hear the sounds of the truck downshifting, easing over the hill to the main road. Then I turned, barely breathing and faced the headstone. On the left their names were carved in block letters. On the right were the dates boldly showing the truth of three lives cut short; one so *terribly* short. A rush of tears streamed down my face. I didn't try to stop them as I landed on my knees. At some point I stopped hearing my own cries and instead, I heard the steady call of the songbirds. Then a scamper of squirrels scratching tree bark could be heard overhead. I also began to hear the soft gurgling of the waters in the creek. Bending over the side I dipped my hand in the cool peaceful flow. Scooping some out with hands cupped, I was able to get back with enough to sprinkle droplets on the headstone. It was an anointing, I suppose—a baptizing. They were home.

~~~

Will Hardy

Eight Years After The Night

When I left Sheriff Jones' office that day I didn't head back to Atlanta. Instead I headed north to Habersham County to meet Mac Blanchard. Mac Blanchard turned out to be a better ally than Hardy ever imagined.

"Well," said Blanchard, with a long emphasis on the vowel sound, letting you know you were in for a tale. "Yessir, I know more about those boys than I'd like to."

I settled into the chair, knowing that this was an introduction and to just sit tight and wait.

"As I recall," continued Blanchard, lifting his hat and reaching to push back the strands of gray hair on his balding head. "There were some tourists who came through here many years ago. Now I remember this because of what they told Jim down at the gas station and then what he told me."

"You see those tourists didn't like the goods being offered to them by a pair down the road from the station. And when they told old Jim at the station, well he was just mad as a hornet! He figured since he paid real rent for real land that he ought to have first dibs on folks up and down that busy road!"

"What were they selling?" I asked, my interest piqued.

"Oh hell! They were selling their grandma if they could! Skins of rabbits and deer, old glass bottles, but the thing that got those out-of-towners talkin' was the jewelry!"

"Jewelry!"

"Yep, the jewelry alright! It was nice, like and all, but that lady thought it didn't quite fit the rest of the goods for sale there, if ya' know what I mean." He looked over at me real serious like.

"So she told the gas station attendant?" I asked.

"Whao, whoa! She told old Jim who owned the station but like I said, it was more like he just didn't want anyone cutting in so close to him. Business is business even up here, Will."

"Why, yes, of course it is," I said, thinking about the criminal element. It's the same everywhere.

"So's old Jim shook 'em down, got a trinket or two for not telling the police, and off he went back to his station."

"So why'd he ever call you," I mused aloud. "That is odd."

"Yes, it *is* odd, that is why I remember it after all these years!" he exclaimed excitedly.

"See, Jim there, he was just letting 'em know who was boss. So when he grabbed up those trinkets with a swoop of his hand, he didn't get a good look at them till he got back, you see?"

"So...what'd he have?"

"Some nice piece, a necklace with a heart surrounded by diamonds. Well not like fancy nice," Blanchard frowned. "But they looked real."

"How'd he know anything about jewelry?"

"Well, you know, he didn't! But what got him thinkin' was the other thing he had. It was a college ring. A college ring from Nevada University, graduating class of 1974.

Yep! The same one that was on that fella who went missing—the very same one."

Hardy whistled low and long. "Well, well."

"Do you still have that file?" Hardy asked excitedly.

"Well now, Will, I had to turn it over to the Feds. You know it became a federal investigation. A *murder*! Them boys up and killed that man from Nevada! For what? A gold ring? So those two Thomas boys went to the Big House!" He finished with a flourish.

"But you kept your file on it, right?" I asked?

"I'd imagine it's somewhere. I took pictures of the jewelry. I think that was just about the time a lot of agencies started using computers. But the pictures....hmm," he tapered off.

Waiting, I took a long breath in. Exhaling, I could see Mac suddenly looking off in the distance.

"Mac, you were saying?" I prodded gently.

"Oh, yes! I was saying!" a startled Blanchard came back around. "What was I saying?' murmured Blanchard as he gazed out the window. After a long pause, I interrupted his thoughts, "Umm, Mac?"

"Hmm?" Blanchard responded, seeming confused. "I'm getting older you know?"

"You look pretty spry to me," I said, although I clearly noticed the age spots darkening his hands, almost making them another color all together.

"Hardy, your day will come, if you're lucky, and you'll get to know for yourself," Blanchard was now smiling, seeming to be back in the conversation. He buzzed his assistant.

"Please get Will here copies of those old records we were talkin' about. Get him anything he wants," Mac ordered.

"Yessir," she answered back. "I'll have to get one of the rookies to go to the warehouse. I'll forward it on as soon as we locate the file."

As quickly as Blanchard pulled it together, his mind would shift again and I could see he had tired quickly. Too quickly. I said my good-byes and promised to come back again and visit soon. I hoped that finding the file wouldn't take too long. The push for speed was nagging, pressing like a chimp hanging on its mother's back.

"Please do come back, Will," Blanchard said looking up from his desk. "When my memory is good it is really good. Today is just not one of those days I guess. It's real nice to have you visit today. Real nice."

"I sure will, Sheriff Blanchard," I said, really liking this guy, and knowing that I would, indeed, come back to visit.

Back in the car, headed south to Atlanta, I called Jenni Ann.

"No, Will, I don't remember her jewelry," she said straining her mind for a memory, a glimpse of her mother in jewelry.

"Aside from her gold wedding band, which she wore every day, I just don't really remember," she said exasperated. "I remember her and can still see her, slipping off the wedding band as she did every night to moisturize away the work of the day."

"Was there ever a necklace, a heart shaped necklace," I prompted.

"Let me think," she said. "Let me close my eyes and see it in my head."

I drove as she thought.

"Oh, yes!" she exclaimed. "An image just came to me. It was an unusual night, because Mom and Dad were going out to a fancy dinner. An anniversary dinner maybe? I don't even know. But she *was* wearing a necklace. A small heart surrounded by little diamonds. Yes! It hung from a gold chain. At least I thought they were diamonds!"

"If they can uncover the pictures then we will take a look for that. Good, Jenni. Real good. I know this is a long shot, but I'll keep at it. Maybe we'll get lucky," I concluded. But just knowing that the Thomases' moves fit in with every timeline—even their absence now made sense! Were they out now? It gave me hope of maybe, possibly, finally, closing this damned case.

On a hunch, I decided to go back to the outskirts of Dahlonega on the ride back south. As I approached a four-way stop I saw Sheriff Jones' cruiser just as it was going through the intersection, heading back towards town.

"Hmm," I thought. "Glued to the desk, huh? I wonder where old Jones has *really* been!"

Following my instincts, I waited. Only fifteen seconds were needed until I was sure the cruiser would be well down the road and out of sight. Creeping up to the four-way and looking in all directions I was reassured of my solitude. Turning, I drove the road that Jones had just come down. There was not one other side street or road on this stretch for miles. The pavement was dotted in potholes and getting progressively worse. The weedy grass encroached slowly on both sides as I continued. Only in one spot, one almost imperceptible spot, did I notice anything: tire tracks in the soft dirt seemingly coming out of nowhere. I cursed myself for not getting the odometer repaired in the old Ford and guessed at the mileage from the intersection as I turned around to go home. I would need some maps and some daylight to follow up on this.

~~~

Jenni Ann

Age Twenty-Five

> *And as he silently roved,*
> *Where evil violently ploved*
> *They knew he'd live or he'd die by the code*
> *Of the Lawman.*

I hummed these words as Hardy's signature ringtone beckoned to me from deep in my purse. I put my paintbrush down to search but I almost didn't want to find my music maker. I wanted to sing the whole song.

"Will!" I said when I finally got my grasp on the tiny phone.

"Jenni," he answered. "Unbelievable! They found the old pictures! And lo and behold there it was! A small heart surrounded by small diamonds on a gold chain!"

"Oh, I want to see the pictures! All of them!" I exclaimed.

"I'll get 'em to you. Maybe you'll remember more if you see the pictures," he said.

"Yeah," I sighed. "Maybe."

"Well, hey, don't be so glum. I'm still poking around up there and I'm going to get those photos from Mac Blanchard today. He says that Jones has not called not even once like he said he would."

"Well, "I responded, "you said from the beginning that he was no good."

"Yeah, I did, didn't I?" he said.

"It's a pretty tight knit group, but Mac, now Mac, he's different. I do believe he will break out with something soon."

"I have faith in you!"

"Speaking of faith and all that, what did you two decide about that wedding? Preacher or minister?"

"I think we will do whatever makes Gloria happy," I laughed. "The very first day of marriage would be a good day to get along with your mother-in-law, don't ya' think?"

"You always were a smart one," he answered. "Okay then, I'll let you know!"

Hanging up, I smile remembering why I even *know* the song "The Lawman." It came from some old television show my father used to watch. I don't recall the show itself except that it was some western. I would be lying on my belly on the floor, drawing. I would slide my feet up and down the side of Daddy's royal blue chair as he would watch the show. As I lift my paintbrush back up to my canvas, I am still humming the tune.

~~~

Will Hardy

Eight Years After The Night

On this visit Mac was having a good day. He began recounting a story with vigor.

"I was brand spankin' new to the force up here, and when I say 'the force' don't go thinkin' it was some shiny squad cars and men lined up in spiffy bright uniforms. No, I mean it was the secretary, me and the sheriff," he laughed. "And I got a badge, pinned it to my freshly ironed shirt and danged if that wasn't the very day that stranger went missing."

"Missing, yes," I perked up, listening.

"You know, it was the darndest thing," he said, his eyes as crystal clear as his mind today. "This stranger had shown up here, asking around and needing some locals to help him with his maps. He said that he knew about the heist of the largest gold coin mint in North Georgia and if we could find it, we'd all share in the reward money from the government."

"That heist took place for sure," I spoke out, having now done my research.

"Yes, well," continued Blanchard, "that is so, but no one thought the gold was still anywhere around here!"

"That's what the report said, too," I concurred. "The one from the Professor Parker."

Blanchard lifted his coffee mug up off of the desk. He took a sip and winced at the apparent foul taste. "That stranger said that some real smart crooks out of Nevada had maneuvered the heist. But they could never get all of the gold out of these mountains. Seems they hadn't counted on the influenza pandemic."

"I read about that one, Mac," I said, now that we were on a first name basis. "It resulted in twenty million deaths, five hundred thousand in the U.S. alone."

"That's right, Will," Blanchard nodded. "Some died right here and some made it out—but without the gold. Seems that they say it is buried around Lumpkin County somewhere."

"Can you imagine if that tale were actually all true?" I mused aloud.

"It seems im-damn-possbile!" joked Mac, accentuating each syllable. He was really having an all-star day and I was happy for him.

"Hey this coffee's old and cold. Let's you and me go get some real coffee across the street," offered Mac with a big grin. "I'll show you the plaque they put up in my honor, for all of my Fifty Years of Dedicated Service to the Georgia Sheriffs' Youth Homes!"

"Absolutely," I said as I stood and grabbed my jacket off the back of the chair. "It would be my honor! But let me just make a few phone calls first."

The first call was to an old friend from the neighborhood.

"Hey there, Sid!" I said.

"Yep, I'm still hunting down the city's most wanted," I answered through the phone.

"And you? You still parceling out and selling every piece of dirt in the country?" I asked while turning to make room for someone passing by in the hall.

"No, no, still no wife, and no kids," I said wondering briefly where that dream had gone.

"And your girls? They are okay?" I continued. We exchanged a few mileposts in the year since we'd last spoken.

"Sid, you are the best damn dirt lawyer in the state, maybe the whole southeast, and I need some help. I need a topography map of a rural Lumpkin County area. Any information you've got would be great! You know, latitudes, longitudes, the works."

"Yes, I know," I acknowledged. "It may not have been surveyed for a long time, but it might even be better if I had some old maps. You can get me what you can, umm hmm, I'd sure appreciate it!"

I called Jenni Ann with the latest update.

"So I'll be back in Atlanta this evening. I should have my sources getting back to me on the road-to-nowhere by then too."

"That's' great!" she answered. "We're up here too, you know."

"Yep," I quickly responded. "And those in-laws of yours are headed down, and your contractors are working, and that is way too many people for me."

"Well okay, okay but if you change your mind..." she trailed off.

"I know and thank you, but you see I'm on a case here, too."

"I know, and it means the world to me that you are. Hey, you know I've got that emerging art scene event this Thursday in Atlanta. Think you can make this one?"

"And you know I'd like to be there," I said noncommittally.

I didn't want to promise. It seemed someone, somewhere always broke some law just as I was heading over to see her latest work.

"One day I will definitely make it over! I will make it over with bells on," I reassured her. "You're not going anywhere."

But wasn't that what she'd thought years ago, about her family, about Abby, about how much time she truly did have? Sid had better hurry, I thought.

No sooner was I back in Atlanta then what I needed was waiting for me on my desk. It was all in my hands. I studied it to get the lay of the land.

"Let's see," I said to myself. "That property is actually the same as this side, over here, on Brushy Mountain. And so, it would seem that they are one in the same, just you can't get from one side to the other without a machete."

My eyes darted back and forth on the map. I knew it was time to put on my boots, turn around, and go right back up to the mountains. To Brushy Mountain, on the backside, down an old road that no one knows about. One that was forgotten over time, omitted seemingly without ceremony. It had to be now.

~~~

Jenni Ann

Age Twenty-Five, The Homeplace

Gloria and Ash flew down the following day as planned. It was the beginning of April and we had less than two months to finish the attic studio and plan a wedding. I had never felt this *whole*, not since before *The Night*. It was noon when Ashton, his parents and I alit from the Suburban and headed to the front door.

"Oh, no!" I frowned. "I think I forgot the dang key!"

"Are you sure?" a concerned Ashton asked. "What about the workmen? How'd they get in?" he asked while I searched and searched my purse, but to no avail.

"I gave them access through the back door and locked the door going to the kitchen," I said in dismay. "Oh, wait! I remember Hardy telling me to take up that key from the cubby! Only I never did!" We all looked until we indeed found the cubby and the key. As we entered, Ashton's parents gave the requisite, oohs and ahhs. Ash set his golf clubs on the front porch, looking forward to conquering the Jack Nicklaus Signature Achasta Golf Course in Dahlonega. We unpacked the rest of the car and got the groceries put away.

"Well, I suppose it's time to see what they are up to in the attic," I stated slightly reticently. As we all climbed the rickety stairs, I called out to my contractor, "Keith? You up here?"

"Hey, Ms. Jenni," he said, reaching down to steady me as I stepped up on the landing. After introducing him to Gloria and Ash, I noticed the windows, long boarded up, now showing sunlit corridors on the dusty floor.

"Oh," I exclaimed, "that is going to make this space even better for my studio! I love those windows and the natural light!"

"Yes, Ms. Jenni," Keith agreed. "Umm, Ms. Jenni? We found these."

We all looked in his direction.

"Kinda odd though," he continued. "We found them boarded up in the rafters."

They were paintings. Three in all.

"But...what? Let me see," I said. I carried one over to the window.

"Bring them over here to the light," I said to anyone and no one. Lined up they seemed so familiar and yet could be scenes from almost anywhere. Were they from here? From the homeplace?

"What in the world?" I contemplated this in amazement.

"Here, Ms. Jenni," said Keith coming over with a cloth, "let's wipe off some of this old dust."

I held out my hand without lifting my gaze from the painting. I swiftly whisked the cloth back and forth over what appeared to be a signature. Could I be seeing straight?

"Lorilei Gold! That says Lorilei Gold!" I said, my throat tightening. "My mother!?"

The style was similar to mine. Not as refined but indeed similar. I spun around and wiped away at each canvas. Yes! Lorilei Gold's signature was there.

"I knew she painted! Not like this! Nothing like this!" I was trembling.

"Look at this!" I exclaimed, now seeing how it might have been. "Each was from the same location, but it seemed as if she had turned, each turn a forty-five degree turn, and then painted again from that angle, until you could see a panoramic view of the homeplace in spring." Excitedly I recalled, "Yes, she had really loved it here in spring!"

It was her favorite time! The lush greens of the leaves to the west side, the vibrant reds of the azaleas near the garden to the north, the yellows of the daffodils and the purple of the crocus's against the sandy reeds of the grasses along the south, but where was the eastern view?

"They look very similar to the mysterious one we got from down here," stated Gloria.

"They sure do," agreed Ash.

"What?" I shook my head, seeing the resemblance, remembering in my mind the unique brushstrokes of the art hung on their library wall. It hit me so hard I felt I was spinning.

"Oh, my God," I exhaled staring at Gloria and Ash. "I think you're right!"

"You mean you think that the actual painting Mom and Dad have was done by your mother?" Ashton distilled it down immediately.

"That seems impossible," Ash gasped.

"I don't know, it seems *possible*," Gloria nodded.

"Let's go," I jumped up. Once outside we scrambled hurriedly to the vantage point.

"Here is where she must have been sitting," I said. We all looked around and down at each painting, pivoting in the place where she surely sat so long ago.

The painting that Gloria and Ash had! It was the eastern view! It had the springtime view of Old Maple, with the creek just behind, and the deep of the woods beyond! Oh how had I not seen this before? A cold sweat came over me.

"Jenni," worried Ashton, "are you okay?" He caught me just as my knees were buckling.

"I'm okay," I weakly whispered as Ashton guided me to sitting. "She sat right here, painting the homeplace in spring, because she loved it here. I was forgetting. Pushing her memory under the rug! I remember now how she loved it here! I don't want to forget anymore!" I cried with joy like a baby who has taken her first steps.

Gloria, with tears all her own, hugged me tightly.

"She and I both love it here!" I choked out the words.

"Well, I'll be damned," Ash said, as he and Ashton again looked back and forth at each painting. Some trees were missing and some were now grown, as a baby to an adult.

I wondered later how one of the four paintings could have been separated from the others. I would learn of the Thomas's chance finding of it during one of their lootings of our home, so many years ago, and selling it as quickly as they would their own souls, on the side of the road.

~~~

Evening

"It is amazing that they've held up so well all these years," said Ashton viewing them again that evening.

"Right!" I agreed looking at them leaning against the fireplace. "You know, they will have to be authenticated."

"I'm sure you know someone perfect for the job," said Ash.

I stood up from the sofa and walked over to the first, touching the corner of the canvas.

"Yes, yes I do," I said quietly. "They'll see what materials were used. It doesn't seem like there is a gesso board but that could just be an amateur thing."

"A gesso board?" questioned Gloria.

"Yeah, it's like a primer," explained Ashton.

"Right," I continued. "They'll look at the canvas itself, the wood used for the frame, the staples..." I said trailing off.

Ashton moved to stand behind me. "And where we found them! That's part of the equation!"

"Yes, yes it is," Gloria chimed in.

"They are fully authenticated in my book," Ashton said. "Fully and one hundred percent!"

As the sun began to set in the sky, Gloria declared it time to start dinner. She did what she does so well and began her own creation of a savory sumptuous feast.

"What a day!" exclaimed Gloria working away at the stove top. "And thank goodness those construction workers are out of here. The dust is incredible! Did you cover the paintings?"

"Yes. I did but I didn't want to stop looking at them!" I answered. I had moved them into my bedroom.

"I had them move the debris out of the hallway too," I added. "It's all outside just by the house. That should make it more bearable tonight."

"That was smart, Jenni," she said, no longer interested in dust and back to the business of dinner.

"You know, you can still go stay in town, there's a quaint bed and breakfast you might enjoy," I reminded her.

"No, heavens, no," she protested, adding with a chuckle, "and miss all the excitement? Anyway, you two would starve if I weren't here."

"You know, Gloria, you are right," I said truly in awe of her cooking. "But seriously, I think you should consider writing a cook book," I said, dipping a small spoon in the sauce she had simmering on the stove.

"Umm," I said, slipping the tiniest bit in my mouth. "I mean, umm, you should really seriously think about that."

As Gloria put the four, rice-stuffed Cornish game hens in the oven, she sighed.

"Oh, Jenni, I'm not much for that kind of thing—too burdensome. Best just to cook it!"

"Oh, my gosh," I brainstormed. "Even better! You could do a TV show!"

"Okay, Jenni, it's been a long day and now I can hear it's taking a toll on you."

"No, really, Gloria!" I said.

"Really what?" asked Ashton as he entered the room freshly showered for dinner.

"Your mom, I was saying she should write a cookbook and then it hit me—POW! She should do a TV cooking show!"

"Yeah, Mom, you'd be great," agreed Ashton, lifting the lid off of a pot on the stove. "Hey, Famous TV Cooking Lady, that smells amazing! What's for dinner?"

"Hey," said Gloria, smacking him playfully on the back with an oven mitt. "Leave that alone, it has to reduce."

"C'mon Ashton, let's get out of her way and set the table," I said, pulling his arm sleeve lightly. Once we were around the corner, I snuggled up to him, "Umm, someone smells even better than the dinner."

We broke our kiss when Ash strode into the room, saying, "I've got to be up at the crack of dawn to meet the rest of the group at the golf course. I don't know them personally but the golf network never fails. You always meet interesting people." He was walking around, his cell phone lifted and pointed it in all directions before muttering, "There's just no service up here."

"Yeah, I know," I said, glancing over at the antiquated black box attached to the wall in the kitchen, its cord dangling below.

"Does anyone have an alarm clock? You know," he joked, "like in the good ole days?"

"I'm sure there is still one around here," I said as I set out to look in the bedroom dresser drawers.

"I'll help," Ashton piped in, following me through the kitchen and down the hall.

"Do we still have to stay in different rooms, I mean really?" asked Ashton as we entered the farthest room where I was sleeping.

"I know it seems silly, but whenever we stay at The Cape, Gloria always has separate rooms for us."

"I know, I know," he recalls.

"We'll be married soon and then that will be the end of that," I said, wrapping my arms around his waist, taking in the strength of him again and wishing for the same bedroom too.

"Cocktails on the porch!" called out Ash. We giggled, feeling as if we ought to hurry out before we are caught in the same bedroom.

"I love your parents," I whispered.

"I love *you*," he whispered back.

The night was cool and the porch rockers were busy.

"You know," Ash started. "Those four paintings needed to be reunited. They need to be together."

"Well, as Jenni said earlier," added Gloria, "they will need to authenticated. But wouldn't it just be *something* if they were all put together?" she said looking over at me.

"Together?" I said aloud, wanting to go back inside and look at the three of them again, to touch them, to smell them to be sure they were real.

"Oh," said Gloria, as she checked her wristwatch and jumped up. "Time to get the hens out."

"May I help?" I asked after her.

"Oh, no, no," she called back to me.

"Do you think she'll ever show me how to cook?" I asked.

"Honey," Ashton said, jokingly, "I believe painting hens rather than cooking them is more your specialty."

"Har de har har, smarty," I answered smiling.

"And yes, Dad, you're right," he added. "We should absolutely have the four paintings together."

The four paintings, I thought to myself, watching as a barred owl swooped over and then continued down past the cedar trees.

Gloria absolutely *could* cook we agreed sitting at the table, rehashing the future ideas of Gloria's cooking fame and the Four Paintings as One. Worn out and full, we all retired for the night. I kissed Ashton goodnight and and headed for my room. I couldn't believe that we found Mom's paintings in the attic. They were so alive and lush. Now I know I am more like my Mother than ever.

The symphony of cicadas and crickets, mixed with a lone coyote's howl, sent us to slumber.

~~~

Earlier that same day Hardy packed his compass, binoculars and a rucksack with some dried fruits and meats. The water belt he would wear had ten different eight-ounce pouches so that it was evenly distributed and if one broke, you didn't lose your entire water supply. Checking the weather report one more time, he was reassured that it would be a mild day. He'd be there by afternoon and he planned on being out of there by nightfall. He got the report that the Thomas brothers were out of prison. The odds were good they were somewhere up in those mountains. The last items on his list were his police assigned revolver and his 9 mm Glock with extra magazines.

All during the drive up, he recalled seeing some movement that day with Jones, across the ravine, vast with ivy and vines and brush. But it was right across from Jenni's place and it was just too coincidental for him. Creeping along that road at two miles per hour, he thought he might never find that old road. He stopped and walked, then started and stopped again. Walking farther, he was looking for tracks in the dirt. Fresh tree branches were draped along the nearly imperceptible entrance, as if to say, WARNING: DO NOT ENTER. They had been used to sweep over the barely perceptible tracks. It seems that someone went to a lot of trouble to keep it hidden. He made his way slowly down a narrow roadway. It was dirt and rock with a canopy of trees above.

Although the days were longer, the sun was steadily getting softer in the sky, dipping lower, and Hardy thought about knocking off for the day.

But I'm so close, he thought, studying the map once more. For Jenni, his mind echoed. This is for Jenni. It took a while for Hardy to get his Ford parked, in the middle of the rutted out road. He figured he would have to back out the whole way to get out.

It was his fortune that he was on foot as he ventured quietly onward. The Thomas boys would have heard his approach and surely shot him dead. As it was, Hardy was stealthy and got a sighting on the two right around the time they were gearing up for the trip across the ravine. Thanking the fine people who make night vision binoculars, Hardy adjusted his eyes. He couldn't figure out exactly what they were saying but he knew it was heated. He heard the coyote howl just about the same time he saw the guns.

The Thomases were on edge and the howling only heightened their tension.

"Oh, hell, we are Thomases and we got this far. We're gonna finish off those Gold's, you understand me!" growled Henry.

"Yeah," said Jake, "when that snotty nosed kid was cryin' up there, she was cryin' for this one, the one like a sitting duck, right through the woods."

Looking over at his brother, Henry's eyes were a mix and disdain and anger. How many years had he put up with Jake? And for what? For the gold, he thought to himself.

"Eight years in the pen for getting that map from the Old Fella and now...now it might be worth it!" Henry seethed.

With renewed vengeance, he spoke through gritted teeth. "We know where the key is, she'll never hear us comin'."

"I think she was alone," offered Jake.

"Yeah, the sheriff said that the houseman was out of town, so there won't be anybody else there to help her," Henry snickered.

"Hey, Henry?" asked Jake. "Shouldn't we check with the sherriff, you know, like he said?"

"What the hell for?" he screamed like an animal before the kill.

"Well, 'cause, you know, I know I'm not the smart one, but if we clear it through the sheriff, we got ourselves covered, right?" stammered Jake.

Henry walked slowly over to where Jake sat, looking down on him. "That damn sheriff's got us covered *now*! So do what I say!"

"Okay, okay," whimpered Jake, as he looked down to the guns resting beside him.

"Well, the only one she ever came up here with before was that guy and he might be with her," Henry thought aloud.

"Yeah," Henry directed. "So load extra bullets, Jake, just in case."

Jake's calloused hands took six hollow point bullets and loaded them in the revolver. Then he loaded another.

"Let's go finish this, then we'll get our revenge, our money and the gold," continued Henry with an evil calmness, his eyes black as coal. "We'll blow that damned addition sky high and dig the gold out where it's buried. We could live like real folks, we could *be* somebody!" he said vehemently. "It is ours and tonight's the night, I tell you!"

Henry directed as if in a fever. "So load up!"

It wasn't even midnight and the moon was full. And, thought Henry, with that crooked ole sheriff covering our tails, it was going work out just right.

Hardy pulled out his cell and he tried to call out. First to Atlanta, then to Mac Blanchard in Habersham. The dry crackle was all the phone gave back.

"Damn," he whispered aloud. He knew that this meant now it was just him. It goes against all police training, to go into a hostile situation without backup. He thought about how far he would have to go to get help. He wondered exactly when did the cell service pick back up? How far down the road? Looking down at his watch, he frowned. Ten o'clock. He knew Jenni was just a few acres away. Raising the binoculars to his eyes, he could see the boys, loading guns and pacing wildly. Storming in was not a good option, so he waited. Grimacing at his soft belly, he knew that his stamina would make all of the difference tonight.

Once the Thomas boys got on the move, Hardy knew he had to follow. He couldn't get back to his car and make it all the way down the mountain and back up the other side before they could get to Jenni. There just wasn't time—he had to follow! Looking up, he silently prayed, "I'm going to need you tonight. Please don't let me down."

~~~

Crossing the ravine through the heavy undergrowth was slow going, but it was nothing the Thomases hadn't done before. The moon was full and as they approached the old deer stand, Henry reminded Jake, "This is where they took our brother. *This* is where they *killed* our brother!"

"Yeah—this is where they *killed* our brother!" parroted Jake.

"And don't forget it, Jake," Henry said, with a hiss. "Revenge is *ours*!" Creeping up to the Gold homeplace was the easy part. Reaching into the cubby, Henry asked, "Where is the key, you bonehead?"

"I dunno," answered Jake bewildered. "It is *always* in the cubby. That's the rules, *always* put it back so no one'll ever know we'd been here," he said from memory like a child in kindergarten.

"We'll have to break in then. The window in the farthest bedroom has a loose hinge," remembered Henry aloud. They step carefully towards the back. While the moonlight was shining brightly on the other side of the house, even at its mightiest it can't reach through the huge oaks that tower above, leaving this side nothing but a dark shadow. The Thomases tripped over the boards and buckets and suddenly everything clattered noisily to the ground. Henry extended his arm out behind him, silently telling Jake to stay still. They waited, crouching low under the window of the very room that holds their intended victim, listening. I woke up and peered out through the window. I figured it must be a raccoon or maybe a bear.

"Okay, Jake, now you do what I say," whispered Henry. I could just hear them directly below my window. I raced quietly out in to the hall and nearly rush through Ashton's door.

"Ashton! Someone is out there! Two of them! I heard them! Oh, god!" Ashton is quick on his feet. "Call the sheriff and wake up Mom and Dad!"

"Wait!" I said in a panic. "What are you going to do?" Ashton was clearly in charge and told me, "Do it now!"

"Oh, hell!" seethes Henry quietly. He sees the window curtain outlined in white as the light is turned on in Gloria and Ash's room.

"There is damn sure more than the girl here tonight," he muttered. While they creep back towards the front, Ashton is watching through the living room window. He keeps the lights off and his silhouette is hidden from the moonlight beaming through. As the two pass under the window, Ashton reaches over and turns the handle to the front door. It creaked a bit but the Thomases didn't notice. They were too busy trying to get away from the back window. Henry tripped over the fallen boards. As he scrambled back up, Ashton sees his opportunity. He reaches in his dad's golf bag leaning on the porch railing and pulls out a nine iron. Henry has his hand on the side of the porch and is preparing for an all-out run when Ashton swings the club mightily and cracks it soundly on his head. Henry goes down, just as Ashton realizes there surely is more than one person. Jake backs away, out of reach.

Reverberations of Henry's mantra keep playing in Jake's head.

"*This* is where they *killed* our brother!"

"Don't forget it, Jake."

"Revenge is *ours*!"

And then his father's words echo between his ears, saying, "They can't have our kin, the land *and* the gold! Get revenge!"

And then, one on top of the other, the words, all the words, all mixed together: "This is where they *killed* our brother!...They can't have our kin....Don't forget it, Jake....Get Revenge!...Revenge is *ours*!"

Jake pulled out the revolver and shoots two quick shots, skimming Ashton's right shoulder. I heard the shots and horror grips me.

"Ashton!" I screamed out, dropping the phone with the sheriff's office on the other end. I ran to the front of the house just as Ashton is retreating back inside.

"Damn!" Ashton said as we both notice the blood coming from his shoulder. Gloria and Ash were standing there, too, barely awake and awash with confusion.

"Get down," he yelled at us all. We ducked as one, two then three bullets whizzed through the window, cracking the glass as it slid forward in hundreds of shards on the floor. Then I hear a voice, urgent, begging from outside.

"Hey, Henry, get up!" Jake is whimpering. "*Get up!*"

Henry? Henry Thomas? I cannot believe that this could be them. But, it must be!

Ashton is wincing back the pain and tries to get the Winchester rifle off the wall. I can see the blood. Too much blood. I have not lifted a rifle in a long time, but I remember Pappy telling me when I was a nearly twelve, It's a Winchester. You just lift it like this, see, and then you can look through the scope and get your target all lined up. I recall his teachings as if he were here right now, talking directly to me. *If it is real close*, I hear him say, *like a bear at the cabin steps, then just grab the double barrel shotgun. A couple of slugs will do the job.*

It's like I am on automatic pilot. Before Ashton can stop me I grab the shotgun where it hangs over the fireplace. Glancing through the window I can see the shadow of a man standing. I open the front door fully and see Jake lift his handgun. He points it to shoot me dead in the doorway. My heart pounds in my chest as muscle memory takes over. Like a dream, I lift and cock the shotgun in one move. My shot hits Jake knocking him to the ground. The kick back shakes me but I don't feel it. I am in a trance, hearing my Pappy tell me again, *If he's real close, two slugs will do the job.* As I swiftly ready the shotgun, Jake, now lying on the ground, again raises his handgun to me. This time I blast Jake, hitting him in the shoulder and knocking the gun from his grip.

Ashton and Ash go past me.

"Get the guns!" yells Ashton to his father. Gloria is at my side as I lower the weapon heavily on the porch.

I don't know how many minutes pass before I hear tires crunching on the roadway. I watch as headlights swing around the curves, showing themselves only when the trees will allow, flickering like an old fashioned picture show. I now see it is a sheriff's car. But there are no sirens. And no firetrucks. And no ambulances. I realize later that I should have thought that very odd indeed.

~~~

"Oh dear, sweet Jesus!" Hardy gasped when he heard the shots. He was having a rough time of it and had to untangle himself yet again from the vines.

"O*h, no, no...* tell me I'm not too late," he angrily spat out, wrestling away from the mountains grasp.

With renewed vigor he set himself free. And then, as if sent by the heavens above, he saw it—a patch of brown dirt. The underbrush was so great that to find a spot of dirt was like finding a needle in a haystack. With the help of the full moon he could see it was a trail.

"Well, I'll be," he muttered in amazement, now following the same trail used just moments before by the Thomases.

As he trotted closer he went down the police force training checklist in his mind. He had no idea who had fired the shots and who, if anyone, was hurt, or worse. He knew he would need the element of surprise. Cresting the hill he was close enough to overhear Jones.

"Now, all of you, turn around and *stay on your knees*," Jones instructed cruelly.

We all turned, kneeling at the front porch steps. Our frightened cries are splintered with fragments of emotion and fear.

"I love you," Ashton says.

"Oh sweet, God my baby," Gloria weeps.

"I love you, too," I gasped.

"Hey, Jones," whimpered Jake. "I'm hurt here and so is Henry. You gotta get us some help."

"Oh, shut up," hissed Jones. "You mongrels couldn't even do one simple job right." Jake winced at his words.

"And now," seethed Jones, "I've got to finish it *for* you. So *shut up!*"

Hardy chose his approach—skipping the front altogether he skirted around back.

This would have to be precise, he thought as he stayed out of the moon's glorious glow.

"You see," Jones elaborated, almost gloating, "I'll tell it like this. I got up here just after you two tried to rob the place—and look what I found! You boys had killed them all! Killed 'em all right here in the front yard!" he laughed uproariously.

"You'll never get away with it!" Ashton spoke out angrily.

"Oh yeah, college boy!" said Jones as he strode over directly behind Ashton.

"Too bad you won't be around to see that I *will* get away with it! And for that remark, I'll kill your lady friend here, then your momma and then your daddy, just so you can see," said Jones, clicking Jake's revolver.

I cried out, "I, please!" just as the shot rang out. The next shot came right after the first but I was still kneeling. Still alive. What kind of cruel horror was this?

"Jenni! Jenni Ann!" Hardy shouted, begging God that he wasn't too late!

And then—the heavy thud of Jones' body hitting the ground.

There was absolute confusion; we all turned to look around.

There he was, half squatting, in his expert shooter's stance, just three yards away at the corner of the house. It was the best sight I could have ever imagined.

"Hardy!" yells Ashton. "Hardy, Thank God!"

"Will?" Jenni Ann asks in disbelief. "Will! Will!"

"Stay there, all of you," he instructed.

"Oh, Lord!" wailed Gloria as Ash reaches over and holds her tight. Ashton and I join them, barely able to stand, shaking while Hardy checks his victim.

"No pulse," he said with some obvious satisfaction. Then he went over by the Thomases and surveys the situation. They are pretty bad off.

"Ashton, come here and help me cuff these two. Jenni, go call my office and talk with Detective Pat Murphy," he ordered. "He'll be waiting and can get the state authorities here to help us." Thankfully, he was squarely in charge.

"Well, it looks like you got hit too there, Ashton," Hardy said, noticing the red trickle of blood that stained his nightshirt.

"Oh, I'll heal," Ashton spoke shakily. "He skimmed me good but I'll heal."

"It takes a real man to take a bullet," he said with just a bit of admiration.

"I'd do anything for Jenni," spoke Ashton, his chin up and his voice proud. "Anything," he repeated.

"Well then," Hardy nodded, impressed, "you are indeed a fine man, Ashton, and she deserves no less."

Then the sirens did come. From every direction. This time, we walked out alive. This time, we won.

~~~

The man who rides all alone
And all that he'll ever own,
Is just a badge and a gun and he's known
As the Lawman.

~~~

Next Fall, The Homeplace

"Gold?" stated Ashton. "Still all buried here? How ridiculous."

"Yep! Hard to believe!" agreed Hardy. "They just wouldn't let go of the tale. You might say they were burning with hatred. You might say they were burning for gold."

Uncle Charles strode over, swirling the colors of the fall leaves under his feet as he passed.

"It's time," he said to Ashton.

"Okay, then," Hardy slapped Ashton's shoulder.

"Ouch," he winced.

"Oh no," an embarrassed Hardy quickly replied. "I thought you were all healed up."

"Ha, ha," Ashton grinned. "Gotcha!"

Charles chuckled. "Oh geeze...get on out of here."

Turning to Hardy they both shook their heads at the young man.

"He's a good one, you know," Hardy said.

"Yeah," Charles answered. "Yeah, I do. And so are you. We are so proud to have a friend like you in the family."

"Well, thanks, but, hey, Charles," said Hardy looking him square in the eye. "I wish you were walking her, you know."

"Hardy," he answered. "It's what she wants and I want what is best for her—that's all I've ever wanted for her. What's best."

Gloria helped me through the front door and down the steps.

"Lizzy is here," said Uncle Charles.

"Oh!" I gasped and then bit my lip. Was I ever glad she'd accepted my invitation after all these years of silence.

"You did the right thing," he said as he gave me a kiss on the cheek. "All she wants is a chance to see you happy."

"Well, Gloria," said Charles with his elbow held high. "May I escort you to your seat? It looks like time!"

The old golf cart pulled up, freshly painted and decorated with wild white trillium.

"A more beautiful bride there could not be!" exclaimed Hardy as he reached out for my hand.

"And you clean up pretty nicely yourself, Will," I joked nervously.

As it turns out the homeplace in fall was the perfect setting for our wedding. Our family and friends were seated in rows of white folding chairs just below Old Maple.

The headstones of my family, all of them, had the best view by design. And that very day two white swans stopped in. I could see them floating gracefully behind the scene as the cart delivered us to our waiting guests. My next painting, I thought, taking a mental picture. And in that painting is Ashton. A lump formed in my throat. This is the day I've waited for all of my life. The day I can again be happy. And whole with love. With a family—my family. There is no greater joy.

We queued to the wedding march music as it lifted to our ears.

"Well, here we go," said a smiling Hardy. A single shiny droplet appeared in the corner of my eye.

"Do not mess up that pretty face," he said brushing it away. "This is your day," he whispered.

Turning, he escorts me to where Ashton stands, waiting, at the edge of the pond, down the aisle.

~~~

Burning Gold, copyright - by Clea Calloway

29144118R00184

Made in the USA
Charleston, SC
03 May 2014